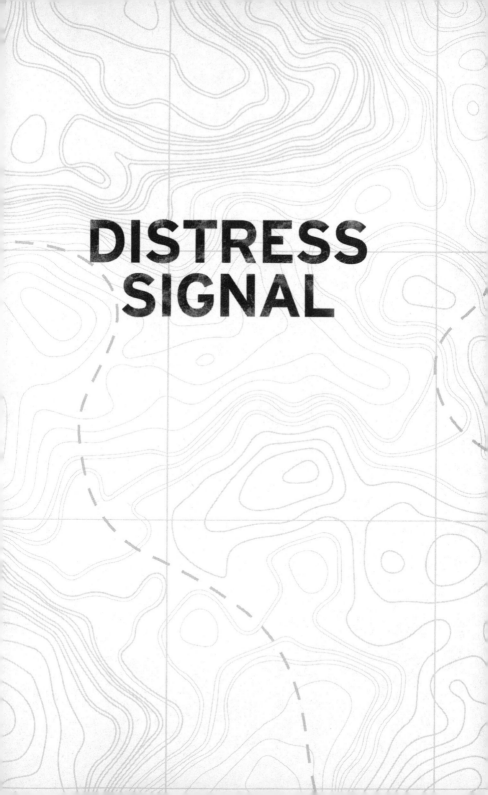

DISTRESS SIGNAL

DISTRESS SIGNAL

MARY E. LAMBERT

Scholastic Press | New York

Library of Congress Cataloging-in-Publication Data

Names: Lambert, Mary E., 1984– author.
Title: Distress signal / Mary E. Lambert.
Description: First edition. | New York: Scholastic Press, 2020. |Audience: Ages 8–12. | Audience: Grades 4–6. | Summary: Lavender and the rest of the sixth graders are on a camping trip to the Chiricahua wilderness, but the trip seems cursed from the start, and when a flash flood splits the group up Lavender finds herself lost, together with her former best friend Marisol, mean-girl Rachelle, and a boy John who has been behaving like a surly jerk since the start—they have only one pack of supplies and only the most basic wilderness knowledge, but if they are to survive they need to put their differences aside and work as a team or all that will be left of them are their sun-bleached bones.
Identifiers: LCCN 2020010995 (print) | LCCN 2020010996 (ebook) | ISBN 9781338607444 (hardcover) | ISBN 9781338607451 (ebk)
Subjects: LCSH: School field trips—Juvenile fiction. | Camping—Juvenile fiction. | Desert survival—Juvenile fiction. | Wilderness survival—Juvenile fiction. | Floods—Juvenile fiction. |Friendship—Juvenile fiction. | Chiricahua National Monument (Ariz.)—Juvenile fiction. | CYAC: School field trips—Fiction. | Camping—Fiction. | Survival—Fiction. | Floods—Fiction. | Friendship—Fiction. | Chiricahua National Monument (Ariz.)—Fiction.
Classification: LCC PZ7.1.L25 Di 2020 (print) | LCC PZ7.1.L25 (ebook) | DDC 813.6 [Fic]—dc23
LC record available at https://lccn.loc.gov/2020010995
LC ebook record available at https://lccn.loc.gov/2020010996

1   20

Printed in the U.S.A.   23
First edition, October 2020
Book design by Keirsten Geise

This book is dedicated to all my favorite ham radio operators:
my grandpa, my dad, my older brother, my younger brother,
and my sister-in-law.
But most especially, it is for our youngest ham,
my nephew, Henry,
and the first girl in our family to get her license,
my niece, Violet.

1

It all started the night of the spring concert.

Looking around, Lavender thought everything was perfect. The stage was decorated with flower garlands of brightly colored tissue paper made by the fifth and sixth graders. In their black-and-white outfits, the choir members looked *sharp*. "No pun intended," John Johnson said when he overheard Lavender say so. Lavender cracked up, but her best friend, Marisol, didn't even smile.

The bake sale was a huge success. John was running the booth at the back of the auditorium with Amy Wright, and they were sold out of everything but oatmeal raisin cookies. Mrs. Henderson, the sixth-grade teacher, told Lavender that they'd raised $279 so far. That, plus the money from their previous fundraisers, would be enough to buy a really nice new telescope for the science campout.

As Lavender took her place on the risers, she couldn't stop smiling. She was in select choir with Marisol, and Lavender couldn't be prouder that her best friend was the soloist. Everyone agreed Marisol wasn't just the best singer in the sixth grade: She was the best singer in the entire school. Probably in the whole state of Arizona.

Mrs. Jacobson raised her baton, and everyone stood a little straighter. Lavender took a deep, deep breath, inhaling until she could practically taste the air . . . and regretted it immediately. The multipurpose room was layered with the stale smell of fish sticks and tartar sauce from that afternoon's lunch, the lingering odor of sweat and volleyballs from that day's PE classes, mixing with the strong scent of fresh coffee, which the PTO was providing for concert attendees. It was a terrible combination. Worst of all, some sixth graders hadn't started wearing deodorant yet, and they really needed it.

Lavender forced herself not to gag. To her surprise, the music teacher was less successful. When Mrs. Jacobson inhaled with the singers, the color drained from her cheeks. As the first notes of the song played, Lavender saw the conductor's baton slip from Mrs. Jacobson's fingers. The teacher clamped both hands over her mouth and dashed for the nearest exit.

Behind her, Lavender heard Rachelle whisper, "I *told* you she's going to have a baby. She's friends with my mom. We've known about it for weeks."

Only Rachelle could be smug at a time like this. Didn't she realize that their entire concert was about to unravel like the Apollo 13 mission? Marisol's solo was supposed to be the highlight of the evening, but unless someone took action, the only thing anyone would remember was that Mrs. Jacobson barfed into a trash can.

There were only seconds left in the song intro. The choir was about to miss their cue. The song would be ruined. Marisol would never perform the solo that she'd been practicing for weeks. Last Saturday, she hadn't even been able to hang out with Lavender because she was working on her piece. This song meant the world to Marisol.

Houston, we have a problem.

Someone had to do something.

Lavender elbowed her way between the snickering

tenors until she was standing in front of the audience, facing the choir. Hundreds of eyes were on her. But there was no time to worry about that. Lavender snatched the conductor's baton from the floor, straightened her shoulders, and as the cue played, she jabbed the baton toward the singers, mouthing the word "NOW!"

A wave of relief washed over Lavender as a handful of voices sang out.

Ordering herself not to shake, Lavender ignored her nerves and concentrated on the music. She waved the baton in an imitation of Mrs. Jacobson, and the faltering voices grew stronger. The members of Wellson Elementary School Choir stopped straining to see if Mrs. Jacobson's head was still in the trash can and remembered that they were in the middle of a performance.

It was working! Marisol would get her solo after all. Lavender felt her shoulders relax. Everything was going to be okay. She held up one hand in a stop signal. The choir paused. Lavender counted a measure and pointed the baton at Marisol.

Her friend's voice, usually so rich and full, quavered and sounded uncertain. Marisol must have been caught off guard by the chaos, which was completely understandable. And even on her worst day, Marisol still sang a hundred times better than anyone else in the choir.

With another wave of the baton, the choir rejoined Marisol, finishing the song. As the last note faded, Lavender lowered her arms. They'd done it.

Thunderous applause echoed off the multipurpose room walls. Lavender beamed at the choir, so happy and so proud of her friend that the corners of her mouth ached with her smile. She tried to make eye contact with Marisol. She wanted a thumbs-up or a wave, but before she could get Marisol's attention, Lavender felt a tap on her shoulder. Mrs. Jacobson stood there, pale but smiling. Lavender could barely hear her music teacher over the roar of the audience.

"Take a bow," Mrs. Jacobson was saying. "You deserve it. You saved the day."

Lavender turned and bowed to the cheers and whistles of the audience, most of whom had leapt to their feet and were clapping for . . . for *her*.

She was a hero.

2

The applause still rang in Lavender's ears as she made her way toward the cluster of sixth-grade girls in the back of the room. She couldn't walk more than three steps before someone stopped her.

"Here's the little conductor!"

"Let me shake your hand. Excellent work, young lady."

"Only a special kid could take over like that."

Parents of classmates, younger students, and even a few complete strangers all wanted to congratulate her for getting the choir through their final song. By the time she reached the back of the room, Lavender had never been more impressed with herself . . . not when she'd won the spelling bee in fourth grade . . .

not when she'd gotten to be the Queen of Hearts in the school play . . . not when she'd gotten first place at the science fair for the third year in a row . . . not even when she'd passed the test to become an amateur radio operator.

Nothing compared to this.

Lavender threw her arms around Marisol. "Wasn't that amazing?" she asked.

Marisol did not hug her back. She stood stiff and awkward for a second before she wrenched herself away from Lavender.

"No, that wasn't *amazing*. It was terrible."

Lavender dropped her arms and took a step back from her best friend. "What are you talking about? I saved the concert. I saved your solo."

"No. You *ruined* my solo."

"But without me, you wouldn't have even gotten to sing."

"That's what you think."

At a loss for words, Lavender studied Marisol's face. Her mouth was an angry, straight line. She was staring at a point on the wall somewhere behind Lavender, refusing to make eye contact and blinking furiously. She looked about two seconds away from tears.

"Hey, Marisol!" Rachelle swooped between Lavender and Marisol, cutting off their conversation. "Your mom asked me to come get you. Your family is leaving now." Rachelle linked arms with Marisol, and the two walked away.

What was happening? Since when were Marisol and Rachelle friends? This simply did not compute.

≈

Lavender tried calling Marisol that night after the concert. She tried again on Saturday and again on Sunday. Marisol did not answer her phone, and she did not call back. By Monday morning, Lavender felt like she was going to explode into as many pieces as two colliding asteroids. They needed to talk.

Lavender's mom explained why Marisol might have been upset after the concert: "You did kind of steal the show, honey."

"Not on purpose," Lavender said.

"I know, but it was supposed to be Marisol's big night," said her mom.

"It still was."

"At the end, everyone was applauding for you."

"I was just trying to help her."

Her mom nodded. "Sometimes, without meaning to, people make things worse when they jump into a situation. It can be really tricky to know the right way to help."

Lavender could understand her mom's point. Sort of. And, anyway, the whole concert thing was over. In the past. There were more important things to think about.

Science camp started on Monday, and as she packed, Lavender had about a billion last-minute questions for Marisol. Which games did she want to play on the bus? Would they rather have almond or pecan granola bars? And what book did they want to read together before bedtime? Lavender wanted everything to be perfect.

This trip was supposed to be the highlight of the year. They would camp for three days in Chiricahua, a vast wilderness in the southeast corner of the state. In her head, Lavender could hear the teacher's voice as she pronounced the word for the class: *chr-uh-cow-uh*. Mrs. Henderson said it was a stunningly beautiful place where different deserts and mountain ranges came together to create a unique blend of landscapes. They would see cacti and pine trees growing next to one another, interspersed with tall rock formations left over from volcanoes that had erupted long, long ago.

Best of all, science camp meant three days of freedom from their normal classes. Three days of eating s'mores. Three days of sharing tents. Three days of nature scavenger hunts and studying the stars and outdoor labs. Science was Lavender's favorite subject. She had been looking forward to this campout since kindergarten.

But even though Lavender waited all weekend, Marisol never called back.

So early Monday morning, Lavender was desperate to find Marisol and smooth things over in person. Lavender waved a hurried goodbye to her dad as he dropped her off at the bus.

"Love you, Lavender," he said.

"Love you, Dad."

"Don't forget about the note I wrote for you. It's in the front pocket of your backpack. I'll be listening on that frequency every night between 7:30 p.m. and 8:30 p.m."

"Uh-huh." Lavender didn't really register his words. Though she'd been looking forward to talking with her dad on their radios, just now she was way more worried about fixing things with her best friend. "Bye," Lavender called over her shoulder as she charged up the bus steps.

Lavender paused at the top, next to the teacher chaperones, Mrs. Henderson and Mr. Gonzales, who sat across from the parent volunteers. Ignoring the adults, Lavender searched for the seat Marisol was supposed to be saving for her. But when Lavender found her friend, she was astonished to see someone else sitting next to Marisol.

Lavender marched down the aisle.

"I'm sorry, but you're in my seat," she told Rachelle.

"I don't see your name on it," Rachelle said.

"Marisol was saving it for me," said Lavender. "You have to move."

"Make me." Rachelle crossed her arms. On her left wrist, she wore a pale pink scrunchie.

Lavender rolled her eyes and leaned over Rachelle. "Come on, Marisol. We'll find another seat to share."

"Actually, I'm going to sit here," Marisol said, looking at her hands as she spoke.

"What?" Lavender had to have heard wrong.

"Hurry up, Lavender," Mrs. Henderson called from the front of the bus. "You're the last one. We're all waiting on you to sit down so we can get going."

Marisol whispered, "I'm going to ride with Rachelle."

This couldn't be happening. She and Marisol did

everything together. Everything. Homework. Group projects. School plays. Even summer camp. Like best friends were supposed to.

"Are you serious?" Lavender asked.

Rachelle rolled her eyes. "Stop being so dramatic, Lavender."

That was ironic. Rachelle was the sixth-grade drama queen, and everyone knew it. Lavender ignored her to focus on what was important. "Is this about the concert?"

"Yeah. And other stuff." Marisol shrugged uncomfortably.

"Lavender, you need to sit down now." Mrs. Henderson sounded as if she needed another four hours of sleep. "There's a spot next to John."

Lavender heard a snort; Rachelle was laughing at her.

"Hurry up," the teacher said, rubbing a hand across her forehead. "I've got an announcement to make."

Lavender could feel the eyes of the entire sixth grade watching her. And not in a good way. She wished the floor of the bus would open up and swallow her whole. With a last glance at Marisol, who still refused to look up from her lap, Lavender dashed down the aisle toward the seat Mrs. Henderson had pointed out. As she plopped into it, Lavender shoved John's giant backpack out of her way.

"Hey, watch it." John grabbed at a strap before his bag could hit the ground.

"Sorry," Lavender said.

"You can't sit here. I need the space for my backpack."

Lavender blinked. Since when was John so rude? Had the entire class gotten personality transplants over the weekend? Sixth grade felt that way sometimes. People were starting to grow up, and it didn't always look good on them.

"Well, Mrs. Henderson told me to sit here," Lavender said.

Before John could argue, Mrs. Henderson clapped her hands twice. "I have a few reminders before we get on our way."

John glared at Lavender and pulled his backpack protectively onto his lap.

While Mrs. Henderson rattled off a list of rules, Lavender replayed her disastrous conversation with Marisol and Rachelle. The more she thought about it, the more Lavender realized that this wasn't the first time Marisol hadn't been herself lately: wanting to switch where they usually sat in the cafeteria and pretending she was scared of a bug in the classroom like everyone else when Lavender knew for a fact that Marisol loved insects. She thought they were fascinating.

Lavender's thoughts were interrupted as Mrs. Henderson suddenly raised her voice and said, "The last thing I have to say is rather unfortunate. So please sit up and give me your eyes. That includes you, Sedgwick. Kyle. Lavender. Sit up. All of you."

Grudgingly, Lavender shifted in her seat and made eye contact with the teacher.

"I am afraid that the money you raised for our telescope on Friday evening has gone missing."

There were gasps from around the bus.

The teacher went on. "When one of the student workers at the bake sale stepped away from the table to use the restroom, the envelope of money disappeared. Though we conducted a thorough search, we were unable to find it. With hundreds of people in attendance, I am sorry to say that it is unlikely we will ever see that money again."

"So there's no telescope for the campout?" Lavender heard her own voice wail above the others. She was already upset that Marisol ditched her. Now this. It was doubly unfair, like spraining your right ankle when your left ankle was already broken.

"What about the other money we raised before that?" Amy asked.

"It was not quite enough to cover the costs of the new one we had picked out. We will put that money toward a new telescope for next year's camp," Mrs. Henderson answered.

Everyone groaned, Lavender included. It was hard to be happy for next year's sixth graders when all her hard work this year was for nothing.

"What about the old telescope? Did we at least bring that?" Raj called out.

"I am afraid the old one was broken beyond repair. But we will still stargaze. Even with the naked eye—" A couple students giggled at the word *naked*. Mrs. Henderson shook her head at the gigglers as she repeated herself more loudly. "Even with the naked eye, you will be able to identify many constellations for your maps, and you will likely see a number of shooting stars."

Meteors. They would likely see meteors, but Lavender was too miserable to bother correcting Mrs. Henderson.

"Who would do something like that?" Lavender wondered out loud.

"Do what?" John asked.

"Steal our money. I can't believe anyone would do that. We all worked really hard to raise that money." She thought about the time she'd spent baking her favorite chocolate cloud cookies with her dad. "Aren't you upset?"

Instead of answering her, John yanked his sweatshirt's hood over his head and slouched over his backpack, giving off all the don't-talk-to-me vibes in the universe.

As the bus pulled away from the school parking lot, Lavender watched Marisol's dark ponytail bob up and down while she talked animatedly to Rachelle. She was wearing a pink scrunchie in her hair. It perfectly matched the one on Rachelle's wrist.

If this morning was any indication, Lavender had a new hypothesis about science camp. It wasn't going to be the highlight of elementary school—it was going to be a nuclear disaster. Level seven.

3

By the time the bus was halfway to Chiricahua, Lavender was wondering if she should try to radio her dad for help. She'd brought her handheld along so they could talk. Lavender's parents thought she was too young for her own phone, and Mrs. Henderson had warned them that they wouldn't have cell reception in Chiricahua anyway, but with the right antenna, a ham radio could work from almost anywhere.

Lavender pulled the radio from the front of her backpack. A few hair ties, a folded-up paper, and a granola bar fell out on the seat between her and John. Before Lavender could pick up any of it, John shoved everything in her direction.

"Keep your stuff on your half of the bench," the world's worst seat buddy said.

Annoyed, Lavender pushed her debris back toward the middle. "This is my half," she said.

"No, this is my side." He brushed it all with his hand, sending a hair tie and the paper scrap toward the floor.

"What's your problem?" Lavender asked.

"What's yours?"

"Pick one. I've only got about a million of them."

John looked up with a startled expression. "Like what?"

As much as Lavender wanted to let her friend troubles spill out, John just didn't seem like he would make a sympathetic ear. She swallowed it back. "You know," she said. "Um, the missing money. All the work we did to organize everything and fundraise, and we still don't get our telescope."

"That's it? If not having a telescope is your biggest problem, then you're fine."

"Really?" Lavender asked. "What's your problem?"

He looked at her, and for a second, Lavender thought he might actually be about to tell her something. Was there a reason he was acting so awful? Then he said, "Nothing. I just wanted to sit alone."

He went back to pretending to sleep. Confused and upset, Lavender picked up her handheld radio. As she tried to puzzle out his behavior, Lavender switched it on and off. On. Off. On. Off.

John had been in her class for years. They didn't hang out a lot or even interact all that much, but he used to be a really nice guy. He never said mean things or picked on other kids. He was smart and athletic and laid-back about most things. She'd even had a crush on him for about a week when they were in fourth grade.

Usually, John played basketball every afternoon with his two best friends, Kyle and Jeffrey. Now Jeffrey and Kyle were sitting at the other end of the bus, while John had transformed into some species of moody hermit crab, hiding in his hoodie for hours at a time.

Maybe he was having friend problems, too.

Lavender started tuning through the frequencies on her radio absently. What would happen once they got to science camp? Would Marisol talk to her at all?

A long, steady beep interrupted her depressing thoughts. Lavender paused on that frequency and put the radio close to her ear.

"The National Weather Service has issued a watch

for eastern Cochise County in southern Arizona. Flash flooding may occur. The flooding is caused by heavy rains occurring ten or more miles away. If flooding is observed, move up to higher ground to escape floodwaters, and report to the nearest law authorities. Repeating: A flash flood watch has been issued to eastern Cochise County until 10:20 a.m. Mountain Standard Time today."

Lavender flicked past the frequency. She had spent her entire life listening to warnings about thunderstorms and dust storms and flash floods. Nothing dramatic ever happened. Phoenix got a monsoon every July and August, but in spite of the warnings on the car radio or her mom's phone, Lavender had never even seen a flash flood.

A shriek of laughter made Lavender look up from the handheld. She peeked over the top of the bus seat. Rachelle and Marisol were shooting their matching pink scrunchies at the guys across from them, and Jeffrey and Kyle were shooting them back.

The difference between them and the hermit crab that Lavender was stuck with couldn't have been more extreme.

One miserable bus ride later, the sixth-grade class of Wellson Elementary arrived at their campsite, unloaded the bus, and set up their tents. That's when the newest disaster struck: Mrs. Henderson "randomly" assigned Marisol and Rachelle to a tent, while Lavender got stuck with Sarah, who was nice enough when she wasn't crying. And when Lavender tried to correct the situation, the other teacher chaperone, Mr. Gonzales, shushed her and said it was time for a group talk from some man who introduced himself as Mr. Bob. Lavender wasn't sure exactly who he was—a campground host or volunteer or something like that. All she knew for certain was that the chaperones expected her to listen to Mr. Bob while he stood on the picnic table and tried to scare the entire class to death.

"So if you do get bitten by a rattlesnake," Mr. Bob was saying, "do *not* tie off the wound. A tourniquet will only keep the poison in one place, and you'll die. You can try to sit or lay down so the bite is below the level of your heart, but you'll probably still die. Your best plan is to not get bitten. If you are bitten by a rattler, start praying and hope to God you get to a hospital in time."

Lavender shuffled her feet and scanned the ground

for any sign of snakes. Yep, she was definitely going to radio her dad and tell him to bring her home. No way was she going to stay out here for three whole days, sharing a tent with Sarah and dodging rattlesnakes like Rachelle. Marisol had clearly been poisoned already. There was no telling who might be next.

From his exalted position on a picnic table, Mr. Bob hitched his khaki pants higher over his gut. Lavender couldn't see his eyes behind his reflective sunglasses.

"Now, I've already told you: No food in the tents, and I showed you how to use the garbage and food storage bins. And why is this so important?

"You there. In the red sweatshirt." Mr. Bob jabbed a finger toward John, who was not volunteering. Lavender waited for the hermit crab to pull his hood back over his face and refuse to answer. To her surprise, he replied.

"Food will attract wild animals."

"That's right. Dangerous wild animals, such as?"

"Rattlesnakes!" the girl standing closest to Lavender shrieked. Sarah was the most nervous person that Lavender had ever met.

Mr. Bob spat in the dirt. "Nope. Unless you're eating mice for dinner. You don't really lock up the food for the snakes." Mr. Bob pointed to John again. "Red sweatshirt, you got an answer?"

"Bears, maybe."

Mr. Bob nodded. He looked over at the teachers and gestured toward John. "You got one smart kid in the bunch."

Lavender bristled. How dare he say there was only one smart kid in the class! Without thinking it through, she thrust her hand in the air.

"Yes, ma'am?" Mr. Bob pointed at her.

"Food in the tents could attract . . ." Lavender tried to come up with a good response. Outside of books and short hikes at South Mountain, she didn't have all that much experience with the outdoors. Lavender knew way more about electronics and astronomy and scientific theory than she knew about camping. Still, she'd grown up in Arizona. She could think of something and show Mr. Bob that there was more than one smart kid in this class. "Um, squirrels and, uh, skunks, or raccoons."

Were there even raccoons in Arizona? Lavender thought frantically. She hadn't ever seen one in her home state, but didn't those things live everywhere? Like cockroaches or pigeons? Either way, she was committed now.

Mr. Bob scratched his belly. "Those are pesky critters, for sure. And you don't want them swarming your camp, but I was asking about *dangerous* animals."

"What if they have rabies?" Lavender asked, feeling smug, because she was sure of herself with this answer.

"You're jumping ahead in my talk, little lady. We'll get to the rabies part later." Now he sounded annoyed, and he wasn't the only one.

As she lowered her hand, Lavender heard Rachelle's exasperated sigh. "She always has to be right, doesn't she?"

Marisol nodded.

Mr. Bob continued, but Lavender had stopped listening. Not by choice. It was like her ears were suddenly tuned to a different frequency and she couldn't focus on anything Mr. Bob said. Marisol had actually agreed with Rachelle. That hurt.

It wasn't true. Lavender didn't always have to be right. She didn't! She was positive she didn't act like that. Marisol never would have agreed until . . . until . . .

Until Rachelle.

This was all Rachelle's fault. Somehow Rachelle

had gotten her fangs into Marisol. It probably happened after Mrs. Henderson put them next to each other on her seating chart. At the time she hadn't thought anything of it, but Lavender could vividly remember Marisol saying that she and Rachelle both liked painting nails and the same music and bubble tea.

Manicures were boring and boba was nasty.

Rachelle was brainwashing Marisol.

Lavender had to remind Marisol who she was and who her real friends were. It was up to Lavender to save her.

"So if you cannot make it to a secure location," Mr. Bob was saying, "and the bear does attack, you fight viciously." Mr. Bob's speech continued in a river of incomprehensible words about throwing rocks and sticks, and giving javelinas—wild pigs—their space, and something about scorpions that Lavender didn't really register.

But in spite of all that, Rachelle was definitely the most dangerous creature in this wilderness. Too bad Lavender couldn't just deal with Rachelle like a wild animal. She would have loved to try throwing rocks and yelling at Rachelle.

Anything to get her friend back . . .

4

"Line up, line up!" Mrs. Henderson shouted. Lavender sat on the campsite picnic bench, staring off into the rocks and mountains that surrounded their campsite. She was trying to think of the best way to get Rachelle away from Marisol. She had to separate them and, somehow, provoke Rachelle just enough to show her true colors.

The other sixth graders swarmed around Lavender. They were scattered across the campsite, hanging out between tents, tossing a football near the picnic benches, climbing on the boulders near the road, and standing on the huge metal food storage boxes on the edge of the site.

"Get down! You're not supposed to climb on those,"

Mrs. Henderson yelled at three students to get off the food storage. "If you want to hike today, line up now."

As the class gathered around the teacher, Lavender twisted a strap on her backpack, wondering if she could pull off some kind of prank on Rachelle.

"Okay, has everyone used the bathroom? Does everyone have their suntan lotion, water, and snacks?"

Lavender nodded, but half the class shook their heads.

Mrs. Henderson groaned. "You have five minutes, and then line up here." She pointed to a spot near the road. "Go on."

Since Lavender had already gone to the bathroom and packed her bag, she stood where Mrs. Henderson had pointed. From her spot, she could hear the two teachers talking.

"Are you sure we should hike today?" Mr. Gonzales asked.

Mrs. Henderson nodded. "Look at these kids. They need to get their energy out, and the weather watch ended hours ago. I'm sure it's fine. There's almost never rain this time of year."

Mr. Gonzales nodded.

Lavender glanced up at the sky. It was blue and clear overhead.

Maybe she could lock Rachelle in an outhouse. Or "accidentally" drop her scrunchie in the fire. Or put a bug in her sleeping bag. Or trick her into thinking there was a mountain lion outside her tent . . . Any of those things would bring out the worst in her, letting Marisol see how awful Rachelle really was.

Footsteps crunching over gravel made Lavender turn around. Rachelle and the scrunchie-war guys were returning from the outhouses. They lined up a couple of feet behind Lavender.

"Are you in for capture the flag?" Kyle was asking.

"Yeah, I guess," said Rachelle.

"Awesome," Jeffrey said. "And you know what else we should do? We should play sardines."

"Sardines?" said Rachelle. "That sounds kind of childish. I haven't played that since, like, third grade."

"We played it at camp last summer," said Kyle. "It's so fun in the woods. Trust me. It's way better in a place like this. If we wait until dark, it'll be really creepy."

"And I'll get more people to join in," Jeffrey added. "The more you have, the more exciting it is."

"Well, I guess I'm in . . . if you guys are," said Rachelle.

"Where's Marisol? Is she gonna play, too?" Jeffrey asked.

"She's still waiting to fill her water bottle," said Rachelle. "But she's definitely in."

Sardines. That sounded perfect. As the class began to walk, an idea took shape in Lavender's brain: a flawless way to deal with a dangerous creature like Rachelle. They just had to get back from the hike and then Lavender would trick Rachelle into thinking it was game time . . . and everyone would see Rachelle for exactly who she was.

The class followed Mr. Gonzales down a dirt path. Mrs. Henderson went to the back of the group and the parent chaperones walked in the middle. At first, the landscape wasn't that different from the campground, but the longer they walked, the more it changed, growing more spectacular with every step farther into the wilderness.

They paused once they reached an overlook. As far as Lavender could see, there were huge rock spires. They looked like massive boulders stacked on top of one another, so high that they nearly scraped the sky.

While the class took in the scenery, Lavender watched Mr. Gonzales and Mrs. Henderson hold a furious, whispered conversation. Each teacher pointed in a different direction. Intrigued, Lavender inched closer, trying to make out what they said, when Amy Wright tapped her on the shoulder.

She held her phone out to Lavender, and for a hopeful moment, Lavender thought Amy wanted to take a selfie with her.

"Will you take our picture?" Amy said, gesturing to Sarah, who stood nearby. After Lavender snapped a few pictures for them, the two started taking goofy selfies. Most of Lavender's classmates were also taking pictures of the rocks and themselves with the rocks in the background. Even John had emerged from the depths of his hoodie to pose with Kyle and Jeffrey.

No one invited Lavender to be in a picture.

Just then, she would have given the most expensive Icom mobile transceiver that money could buy to grab her friend and capture the moment like everyone else. Usually, she was in all of Marisol's pictures, but Marisol was taking pictures with

Rachelle, and she hadn't even looked in Lavender's direction.

Longing to look as busy and important as the rest of her class, Lavender started fiddling with her radio again. With a click she turned it on. There was only fuzz.

Click, she changed frequencies.

Fuzz.

Click.

Fuzz.

Click.

"The National Weather Service has issued a warning for eastern Cochise County in southern Arizona until 5:30 p.m. Mountain Standard Time." She'd landed on the same frequency as before. "Flash flooding was observed in the area at 3:07 p.m. The flooding is caused by heavy rains occurring miles away. This excess of rainfall will cause flash flooding to occur in eastern Cochise County, Arizona. If flooding is observed, move to higher ground to escape floodwaters. If flooding is observed, report to the nearest law authorities. Repeating: A flash flood warning has been issued to eastern Cochise County until 5:30 p.m. Mountain Standard Time today."

Lavender searched the sky. It still stretched blue in almost every direction. On the distant horizon, she could see a few dark clouds, but that had to be really far away . . . Still, Lavender thought maybe should say something to one of the chaperones about the warning, since the National Weather Service had changed the time of the possible flooding from the original announcement that she'd heard earlier on the bus. As she edged closer to the teachers, Rachelle suddenly pointed at her, calling out, "What is *that*?"

Lavender whirled, expecting to see a snake or a bear or, at the very least, a skunk. There was nothing behind her.

"No, what are you holding?" Rachelle asked. "Is that some kind of phone for dinosaurs?"

"It's called a ham radio," Lavender said, shooting a look at Marisol, hoping she would speak up. After all, Marisol had been really excited for Lavender when she passed her test and got the license required for anyone who wanted to be an amateur radio operator. Lavender had even convinced Marisol to try and get her license, too. Once Marisol passed the test, they were going to talk over their radios and do contests together.

Marisol didn't say anything.

Rachelle laughed. "A *ham* radio? That's perfect."

"What?" Lavender didn't get the joke.

"'Cause you're an attention hog. Ham. Hog. Get it?" Rachelle asked Marisol. When Marisol still didn't answer, Rachelle spoke again. "What? Don't look at me like that. You said it yourself. After the concert."

"Did you really say that?" Lavender whispered. An ache grew in her stomach.

Rachelle snorted. "Oink, oink."

All thoughts of the weather warning forgotten, Lavender snapped the radio off. She tried to think of something to hurt Rachelle the way she was hurting. "Yeah, well. Well, you're short. You're so short Castles N' Coasters won't even let you on the big-kid rides."

Rachelle crossed her arms and scowled. "Oh yeah, your—"

But her retort was interrupted by Mr. Gonzales, calling out, "This way, everybody!"

He and Mrs. Henderson started herding the class downhill. Lavender stood there still tingling with shock and anger as Marisol took off, followed immediately by Rachelle. Lavender trailed behind them.

She couldn't wait to get back to camp and get even with Rachelle. She was so distracted, imagining how Rachelle would react to the prank, that Lavender barely noticed that the sandy slope they'd been following was getting wider and wider. Steep hillsides dotted with boulders rose on either side of them. Lavender had no idea how long they'd walked before Mr. Gonzales came to a complete and sudden stop.

He looked all around in every direction, and then he said, "Let's stop for a minute. I think we're lost."

5

Lost? **What else** could go wrong?

Lavender should have turned off her alarm clock, refused to get out of bed, and skipped science camp. Now she knew. When she grew up and became an astrophysicist, Lavender was going to invent a time machine, go back to kindergarten, and tell her five-year-old self, "Don't waste years of your life looking forward to science camp. It's the worst."

"I knew we should have gone the other way," Mrs. Henderson said.

Mr. Gonzales glanced around, consulted his phone, looked up again, and said, "I don't have a signal, so I can't get a detailed map. I'm not even sure this is a trail. I think we might be in a wash. When's the last time anyone saw a trail marker?"

Lavender knew even from small hikes around South Mountain Park in Phoenix that trails were sometimes difficult to follow, and something like the sandy bottom of a wash could easily be taken for a path through the desert.

Mrs. Henderson clapped her hands, and the sound echoed off the rocks around them. "Listen up!" The students fell silent. "We're going to have to backtrack. It appears we've gone the wrong way, but first we'll have a short rest. Find a good spot to sit down. Drink some water. Eat your snacks."

Lavender wanted to stamp her foot with impatience. This was a waste of time. The sooner the hike was over, the sooner she could put Rachelle in her place and get her friend back. And Lavender wasn't the only one upset by the latest development. Her randomly assigned tentmate was in the middle of a full-blown meltdown.

"But we're lost!" Sarah was wailing. "Are we going to die out here?"

Mrs. Henderson was shaking her head and saying, "Calm down. We're going to be just fine. I know exactly where we went wrong. Don't worry."

"Wanna join hacky sack?" Jeffrey popped up from behind to ask Lavender.

"Do we have enough time for that?" Lavender asked.

"Yep, Mr. Gonzales said so."

And just like that Lavender was hit with a sudden stroke of genius. She knew exactly how Galileo must have felt when he discovered the craters on the moon.

"No, thanks." Lavender smiled at Jeffrey even as she shook her head.

If there was time for hacky sack, then there was time for sardines. Forget about waiting to get back to camp. Lavender could get even with Rachelle now.

Her target was standing alone, in the middle of the sandy clearing, snapping pictures. Marisol was perched on a rock a few feet away, sharing a bag of trail mix with Amy. Everything was perfect. Pasting a huge smile on her face, Lavender bounced over to Rachelle.

"Ready to play sardines?" Lavender asked as she zeroed in on the friend thief.

"Are you talking to me?" Rachelle looked up from her phone.

"Yeah, Jeffrey asked Mr. Gonzales. He said there

was enough time for a game." Technically, it wasn't a lie.

"What are you talking about?"

"Sardines. I'm going to play."

"Who invited *you*?"

"Jeffrey."

"Seriously?"

"Yeah. He said the game is more fun with more people."

"Depends on which people."

Losing her temper and almost forgetting that there was no real game of sardines, Lavender snapped, "We're playing with or without you. Are you in or not?"

Rachelle glanced around the canyon. "They said the game is most fun after the sun goes down. It's not dark yet."

"Look at all the great places to hide. You can go way down there, out of sight. This will be even better, because everyone already explored camp, but no one knows what's out here."

Rachelle bit her lip and considered the matter. "Is that what Jeffrey and Kyle said?"

"They're the ones who sent me over here. Sardines was their idea in the first place, wasn't it?" The words were starting to taste like sand in her mouth. Lavender didn't like liars, but it had to be done. No matter how guilty she felt. You couldn't win a war without getting your hands a little dirty.

Rachelle glanced over at the hacky sack game. "Are you sure they said now?"

Trying to keep her expression innocent, Lavender nodded, even as she crossed her fingers behind her back. "They're just going to play hacky sack until it's time to split up and find you."

"Okay. As long as I'm It first."

"That's the plan," said Lavender. She felt guilty, because it was even easier than she'd thought it would be. The perfect prank: simple and elegant.

While Rachelle was out of the way, Lavender could finally talk to Marisol alone. They could apologize for the whole pointless fight after the concert. And then Rachelle would lose her mind when she realized that she'd spent the whole break hiding when no one was even looking for her.

Lavender could picture how Rachelle would scream and shout and call names, and everyone in their class—even the teachers—would see exactly how mean and bratty and awful Rachelle truly was. Marisol wouldn't ever let herself get sucked into

Rachelle's orbit again. So what if they both liked scrunchies and singing? There were more important things to consider. Like years of friendship and all their future plans. Lavender and Marisol were going to go to the same college and be roommates, and then they were going to live on the same street. They had planned it all out when they were in third grade.

"You sneak away and hide," Lavender told Rachelle. "I'll get Jeffrey and Kyle and everyone to start looking for you in two minutes. But you have to be patient. In a place like this, it might take a while for anyone to find you."

"I hope Jeffrey finds me first." Rachelle smiled.

"Why?"

"He's cute," said Rachelle, rolling her eyes. Lavender knew it. Rachelle really was a weirdo. Then Rachelle shouted, "MARISOL! Get over here."

Marisol hopped up and, still carrying her Nalgene, jogged over to Rachelle.

"What's up?"

"We're playing sardines now," Rachelle said. "Wanna be my partner? I'm hiding first. Lavender will tell everyone when it's time to start looking for us."

Lavender felt like the ground was crumbling beneath her feet. "What? We're not playing partners."

"It's more fun this way," Rachelle said. "I'm not going to hide by myself. That would be boring."

Lavender floundered for a way save the situation. "But, Marisol, don't you want to stay here with me?"

"No," said Marisol. "I'll hide with Rachelle. Hiding is always more fun."

Lavender felt the corners of her mouth pinch together. "More fun than looking with me?"

Marisol didn't answer.

"I'll leave this here," Rachelle said, shrugging her backpack off. "It's too bright. It'll give our hiding spot away."

"Okay, I'll leave mine, too, but I'm bringing my water bottle," Marisol said. "I'm still thirsty."

"Good idea." Rachelle clipped her kid-sized Hydro Flask to her belt.

How could Lavender's plan have fallen apart so quickly? She'd thought it was foolproof.

"Don't watch which way we go," Rachelle called over her shoulder.

"Whatever," said Lavender, bending to pick up a

rock. Rachelle did not respond. She and Marisol were already disappearing around a bend in the wash. Lavender longed to throw the rock at Rachelle like she was a pesky skunk wandering into camp, but she knew she couldn't do that. Instead, Lavender threw the rock as hard as she could against the closest boulder. It ricocheted at an odd angle and flew a few feet to the right. No one was nearby, so no one was hurt. Not physically.

6

Well, let them go. Rachelle and Marisol could spend the break squatting together under some bush. If Lavender couldn't use the time to win Marisol back, she would at least prank the both of them.

Lavender slung another handful of pebbles and plopped down on the nearby boulder. Marisol was changing. Lately she was more interested in doing her hair than in classifying insects. Lavender didn't even know if Marisol still wanted to be an entomologist. She talked more about starting a music channel on YouTube than about becoming a scientist. Lavender pulled the last of her trail mix out of her backpack and started chewing a handful of it with unnecessary force.

Sedgwick appeared out of nowhere.

"Brandon told Mrs. Henderson you were throwing rocks, and Mrs. Henderson told me to tell you not to throw rocks."

"Mm-hmm," Lavender answered. Her mouth was full of raisin, peanut, and melted chocolate, and she wasn't in the mood to talk to anyone.

"Want to play hacky sack?"

"Not really." Without looking at him, Lavender took another giant handful of trail mix.

Sedgwick didn't take the hint.

"Do you know what a wash is?" he asked.

Lavender scrunched her face up at his random question.

"Mrs. Henderson keeps saying that Mr. Gonzales led us straight into a wash," he explained. "I don't know what that means."

Lavender couldn't resist explaining. She stuffed her empty bag of trail mix back in her backpack. "A wash is like a dry stream. When it rains, all the water runs off into washes and fills them up . . ." Her voice died out.

A terrible thought occurred to her. Washes were the most likely places to get caught in a flash flood. Every time a scary story came on the news about day-trippers or tourists getting caught or killed in a flood, Lavender's mom would shake her head and talk about how dangerous hiking in Arizona could be.

"Sedgwick," Lavender said slowly, thinking back to the warning she'd picked up on her radio. "Do you know what county we're in?"

"Uh, this is A-mer-i-ca," Sedgwick said.

"No. County, not country."

Sedgwick shook his head, looking baffled. Lavender's mind was racing faster than an electrical signal along a copper wire. On the off chance that there really was a flash flood, the class was in the worst possible place. Lavender grabbed her backpack and pulled it on. Before she could get away, Sedgwick pointed and asked, "Aren't you going to use that strap?"

He *always* buckled the waist strap on his backpack.

"Sure, Sedgwick, whatever." Lavender clipped the waist strap as she made a beeline for the closest teacher. Sudden anxiety was gnawing at her insides. Mr. Gonzales was playing hacky sack with a group of students.

"Mr. Gonzales!" she called out, startling him into dropping the ball.

An annoyed expression flitted over his face. "What's up, Lavender?"

"What county is this?"

Instead of answering, he gave a very grown-up smirk. "Why the sudden passion for geography?"

"Just tell me."

"Cochise."

"Are you sure?" Lavender asked.

He nodded. "I might have gone off the trail a little, but give me some credit."

Lavender's heart rate shot up. "I think we need to get out of here."

"Why?" Mr. Gonzales asked.

Lavender reached in her bag, found her radio, and flicked it back on. The National Weather Service was still repeating the same warning.

Mr. Gonzales listened, rocking back and forth nervously. "They extended it? When did they do that? It was supposed to end this morning." As the announcement started over again, he suddenly broke up the game, waving his arms at the students and shouting, "All right, round everybody up. We've got to get out of here. We're climbing those rocks. This way, everyone."

"Shouldn't we backtrack?" Lavender asked. "Isn't

that the safest way to find our trail without getting lost, like, for real?"

"That was a warning," said Mr. Gonzales. "Not a watch like they had this morning. A warning means a flood either has already been spotted or is imminent. We have to take it seriously."

"But it's not even raining."

"It could be raining miles and miles from here and a flash flood could come down a wash like this." Mr. Gonzales glanced toward the distant clouds. "It's just a precaution. But these things are unpredictable. You know what they say: Better safe than sorry. Come on, let's get everyone moving. Now."

A little spike of fear shot through Lavender. She wished that she'd known the difference between a watch and a warning sooner. She wished she'd asked sooner about the county. The class never should have ended up down here. Her hands shook as she jammed her radio into her backpack.

"Okay, listen up!" Mr. Gonzales raised his voice even louder than before. "I want everyone to get to higher ground. Let's go. This way. We're going to do a little rock climbing."

"What in the world is going on?" Mrs. Henderson called from the other end of the wash.

"Flash flood warning came over the radio."

"What radio?" Mrs. Henderson asked as she started walking in their direction. Then she gave her head a little shake before saying, "Never mind. Not important now." As she neared Mr. Gonzales, Lavender heard Mrs. Henderson ask, "Do you really think we need to climb out of here?"

He nodded, and after a few more whispered words that Lavender couldn't quite catch, Mrs. Henderson dragged Sarah toward the rocks at the side of the wash. Lavender tuned out the commotion around her—Sarah's wails, her classmates' questions, the parent volunteers' orders—and concentrated on climbing up the steep slope until the sound of feet sliding over gravel and a short, sharp yelp grabbed her attention.

Lavender whirled around just as Kyle landed, smashing his knee into a rock. He must have slipped on the loose ground.

Amy and Jeffrey were closest to him. Jeffrey pulled Kyle up, and even from a distance, Lavender could see the blood running down his leg. Amy offered him a hand, and between the two others, he started limping after the rest of the class.

Lavender's heart pounded as she scrabbled up the

rock, watching her footing closely. No matter that Mrs. Henderson was repeatedly telling Sarah that flash floods were "incredibly rare" this time of year, Lavender wanted out of that wash, and she wanted out now.

Mr. Gonzales was shouting encouragement at the students; all the while, he kept pausing to count the class as he made his own way up the rocks. To calm her thundering heart, Lavender started trying to count her classmates, too. *One, two, three . . .* At *eleven*—Marisol's favorite number—Lavender abruptly broke off. They were going to be two kids short when they finished counting.

Rachelle and Marisol were still hiding.

They didn't know about the flood warning.

Lavender had lied, and they were in danger because of it. She had to go get them before anyone got hurt. Before anyone found out what she'd done.

7

Without stopping to look, Lavender leapt from the rock where she'd been standing. She felt her heart soar into her throat as she fell farther than expected. Lavender landed on loose dirt and shifting gravel, and like Kyle only a few minutes before, her feet skidded out from under her. The ground rushed toward Lavender's face. But before she wound up with a mouthful of rock, an arm shot out of nowhere and caught her.

"John?" she asked in shock. She hadn't seen him at all.

"Watch it," he said. "You could have killed us both."

"I'm sorry. I'm sorry." She tugged her arm out of his grip. There was no time to talk. "Be right back," she yelled as she went sprinting and stumbling between boulders. By some miracle, she made it to the bottom of the ravine without landing face-first on a barrel cactus.

And that was when she heard it. Over her own gasping breath, there was another sound. A low rumbling noise.

Was it her imagination?

Could it be far-off thunder?

Or was it rushing water?

Lavender broke into a run again, willing her legs to carry her as fast as they possibly could. She felt like she'd sprinted a mile before she reached the curve in the wash where Marisol and Rachelle had disappeared.

"Marisol!" she called. "Rachelle! Where are you guys?"

Silence.

Then crunching footsteps. "Get back here!" a familiar voice called.

Lavender whirled to see John chasing after her.

"Are you insane? What do you think you're doing? You don't run into a wash in the middle of a flash flood warning."

"Marisol. Rachelle." She half screamed, half tried

to explain: "They're hiding. Not with the class."

"What?" John's mouth dropped open in shock. "Why?"

Lavender didn't even try to answer him. Another low rumble caught her ear.

"Do you hear that?" she asked him, unsure if it was real or if she was hearing things. Like the rush of blood in her own head.

"Hear what?"

Panic growing, Lavender ignored him and started yelling for her friend again. Only this time, she didn't bother to form words. Lavender just let out the loudest, shrillest scream possible. She shrieked like she was trying to win first place in a shouting contest . . . like she had just seen the scariest movie ever made . . . like she was being attacked by a supervillain . . . like her best friend was about to die.

John's voice echoed under hers.

For a second, she worried that it wouldn't work. That Rachelle and Marisol would stubbornly refuse to leave their hiding spot, thinking that this was all some twisted part of the game. But no. Her unearthly scream did the trick.

A nearby bush started to shake, and then Rachelle emerged, followed by Marisol.

"What is wrong with you?" Rachelle planted a hand on one hip and narrowed her eyes at Lavender.

"Flood. Warning. Have to leave. Now." Lavender could barely think straight. Her brain felt scrambled. She was having trouble catching her breath, and her voice was hoarse; her throat was raw after screaming like that.

Marisol glanced down the wash and then finally, for the first time since the concert, she looked Lavender directly in the eye. "Are you serious?"

Lavender nodded.

"Yeah," John said, in a surprisingly steady voice. "We really should go. Just in case. Everyone else is already climbing out of the wash. Come on." He started jogging back toward the class. Lavender followed close on his heels.

They'd only gone a couple of steps, when there was a thunderous crash. A wave of blackened debris-filled water rushed toward them around the distant bend.

The flood was real. It was happening. A wall of water was coming to sweep away everything in its path. Including the four of them.

≈

"Run!" Marisol was the first to react. She spun around and sprinted away from the coming water. John,

Rachelle, and Lavender raced after her, running in the opposite direction of their classmates. The coming flood was between them and the others.

Lavender scanned the ravine. They had only seconds to act. They'd never outrun the flood, and there was no way out of the canyon. The walls were steeper here than on the other side of the curve. "We're trapped!" she shouted.

"Tree. We have to climb the tree," Marisol gasped, pointing toward a nearby mass of sturdy but tangled branches.

Marisol was still finishing the words as John reached the tree, grabbed hold of a branch, and launched himself upward regardless of the giant backpack he wore. Marisol threw her water bottle strap over her shoulder and followed John into the tree. In the same instant, Lavender hoisted herself onto the lowest branch.

The rumble of rushing floodwaters grew to a roar as the wall of dark water crashed toward them. Over the roar, Lavender heard something else.

"Come back down. I need a boost! Help!" Rachelle screamed.

Rachelle was hopping around like molecule in hot water. Her arms waved frantically, but her fingers just scraped against the bottom of the branch. Rachelle wasn't quite tall enough to reach the tree limb.

"There's no time!" Lavender breathed.

There wasn't. If Lavender went back down, they would both get caught in the flood.

Rachelle's eyes darted around the canyon as if she was looking for another escape route, but there was nowhere to go. Mouth gaping open, her skin lost all its color.

Lavender's pulse hammered in her ears and drowned out Marisol's screams as she imagined Rachelle getting swept away.

She couldn't let that happen. Not even to her worst enemy.

Without pausing to think it through, Lavender tucked her feet under a smaller branch. She could only hope it would hold—if it snapped, Lavender and Rachelle were both going to drown in that relentless, churning wave. Trusting both their lives to one slender branch, Lavender threw herself backward.

The branch held. Lavender hung suspended upside down. She'd done this a hundred times on the playground monkey bars. But never from a tree. Never during a flood. And never while wearing a backpack. She could feel the weight shift, but the waist strap held things in place. Lavender would have to thank Sedgwick. If she ever saw him again.

Hanging upside down, Lavender laced her fingers together and shouted at Rachelle: "Step on. Here's your boost. Climb up. Hurry!"

With a speed born of panic, Rachelle thrust a foot onto Lavender's intertwined hands and latched on to the tree branch. Rachelle's legs flailed as she fought to pull the rest of her weight into the tree.

The metal water bottle hanging from Rachelle's belt thumped into Lavender, and one of Rachelle's feet collided with Lavender's stomach. "Careful," Lavender coughed, but as she saw the water was only a few feet away, she added, "I mean, hurry! Hurry!" The urgent words scraped her still-raw throat.

Rachelle's foot collided again with Lavender's abdomen as Rachelle twisted and writhed, pulling herself completely onto the branch. "Oooff," Lavender said as the pain radiated.

Then Lavender saw something dark fall past her line of vision and she screamed—but no, it was something small. Rachelle was safely on the branch above her.

Everything was happening all at once. Lavender finally knew what people meant when they spoke of their lives flashing before their eyes. It had happened in a matter of seconds, but to Lavender, each one of those seconds held an eternity.

Straining her muscles, Lavender yanked herself upright to safety.

"My phone! It fell!" Rachelle was wailing. She had flattened herself on the branch, her arm reaching down and swiping toward the ground, even though her phone was nowhere within reach.

"Stop it! You're shaking the tree," Lavender ordered, but Rachelle had lost all touch with reality. She remained flat on the branch and clawed uselessly at the air even as the water slammed into the trunk.

8

Lavender screamed again. The force of the flood shook the entire tree. She could hear the others shrieking, too. Rachelle clung to the branch, arms and legs wrapped around it like a terrified sloth.

"We're gonna die. Are we gonna die?" Marisol was shouting. She was clinging for dear life to a branch just above the one Lavender and Rachelle shared.

"Maybe," John's voice floated down. He sounded sick.

Rachelle whimpered, "My phone's gone."

Lavender couldn't speak, couldn't move. She saw only the churning water. The flood was dark, full of rocks, branches, logs, and even a few smaller trees being towed by the sheer power of the current. It made her dizzy, and she squeezed her eyes closed.

Something crashed into their trunk, and again the tree shuddered.

"Hold on!" John shouted unnecessarily. Lavender was already hugging the trunk of the tree so tightly that the bark was going to be permanently imprinted on her arms and left cheek.

"Is the tree going to fall over?" Marisol cried. The same hideous thought was occurring to Lavender. After all, she'd just seen trees careening down the river. If theirs was also knocked over by the force of the water, they were goners. Lavender heard herself whimper.

"I guess it could fall," John said in that reassuring way of his.

Rachelle let out a sob, and Lavender risked opening her eyes a fraction. This was a new side of Rachelle, one that Lavender had never even imagined. Rachelle was always in control, always bossy, and often mean. But now, when she and Rachelle were in the same deadly situation, stuck in a tree and seconds from drowning in a freak flood, Rachelle looked as vulnerable as Lavender felt: less of a vicious wild animal and very, very human.

"I don't think this tree will fall. The ones going by

are a lot smaller. Everything will be okay." Lavender tried to shout something comforting to Marisol, and if it made Rachelle feel a little better, that was fine, too. The problem was Lavender didn't know if she believed her own words.

No one answered her. There was only the roar of the water.

≈

Lavender never knew how long they sat in the tree, in sickened silence, watching and waiting for the water to recede. Never in a quadrillion years could she have imagined that, someday, she would wait out a flash flood stranded in a tree on a branch with her archnemesis.

As the water slowed from a crashing, thundering tsunami to a steady, running stream, Rachelle carefully moved into a sitting position. "Are you guys still up there? Are you okay?" she called out to Marisol and John.

"Fine," said John.

"Still alive," Marisol shouted down. "Are you all right?"

"Sort of," Rachelle called. "My phone's not."

"Are you serious right now?" Lavender's heart felt like it was still beating at three times its normal rate. "Are you really worried about your phone at a time like this?"

"How else are we going to get help?" Rachelle answered. "Did you think I only cared about it because it was a brand-new iPhone?"

Lavender blinked in surprise. That was exactly what she'd thought.

"Doesn't anyone else have a phone?" Rachelle wailed.

"Mine was in my backpack," Marisol answered. "I left it with the rest of the class."

"I already tried mine," John said. "No signal."

"Did you try calling 911?" Rachelle asked.

"No, I tried to order a pizza," John said.

In spite of the flood and the fear and the potential death, Lavender laughed. Recklessly. Hysterically. But still, it was a laugh.

Rachelle didn't see the humor. "Shut up," she snapped at Lavender. "You don't even have a phone—just some walkie-talkie from the Stone Age."

Her radio! Lavender couldn't believe that she hadn't thought of it sooner. To be fair, she'd been a little distracted by their brush with death and all that.

"Oh my gosh! We're saved," Lavender shouted. Still hugging the tree trunk with one arm, she swung her backpack off one shoulder and into her lap, then pulled out her radio. With it, she could call for help. She just had to tune through the frequencies until she found another operator. Then she could explain the situation, help would be contacted, and someone would come get them.

In fact, with her radio, the four of them might be the first ones to make it back to camp . . . way before the rest of the class. Lavender knew that very few of the students had a cell signal at camp and that no one (including the teachers) had had cell service once they'd started their hike.

Lavender clicked on her little radio. She heard only thick static and empty air.

She held down the talk button and said, "Mayday."

No answer.

"Mayday. Mayday."

No answer.

Lavender remained on the frequency several minutes before moving to another frequency. "Mayday, Mayday." She tried again and again, continuing to move from frequency to frequency.

Lavender was already feeling hopeless, when Rachelle said, "Do you have to keep doing that? You're making me more nervous."

"Do you want to be rescued?"

"I don't see any help coming."

Lavender wanted to throw her radio at Rachelle's head, but she wasn't picking anyone up now anyway. Maybe she should put it away and try again later. She was completely caught off guard by the sudden lump in her throat. She'd been so sure that she had the perfect solution to their dilemma. Now what?

"Please don't fight," John said in a strained voice. "Lavender's trying to help."

Rachelle said, "She's only making it worse, yelling 'Mayday, Mayday' every two seconds."

Lavender waited for Marisol to defend her, but of course it didn't come.

As the endless seconds ticked by and Lavender's heart slowed to its normal speed, she began to notice just how uncomfortable she was. Her butt hurt. Her legs hurt. Her back hurt. Sitting on a high branch was fun for a few minutes, but not in a flood and definitely not after what felt like hours.

At least the flow of water had stopped, and the ground was transforming into a patchwork of puddles. It almost looked like it might be possible to climb down, though Lavender was still worried that a branch could come around the bend in the canyon and knock them off their feet if they tried to wade to safety.

Spots of dried ground began to appear, and the late-afternoon sun was casting long shadows, when Rachelle announced, "That's it. I'm going down."

"Wait, what?" Lavender asked.

"The water is almost gone. The flood is over."

"I know it looks that way," Lavender said, "but what if it's not over? What if there's more coming? Don't you think it's safer to stay up here for a little longer?"

"Why? There are only puddles left," said Rachelle. "It's a *flash* flood. That means it's over in a flash, and we've been waiting forever."

"Actually," said Lavender, "I think it's called a flash flood because it comes out of nowhere."

"Whatever. Who even cares?" said Rachelle. "You can do what you want, but I'm not spending the night in a tree."

"It's too dangerous," Lavender said. She didn't have any desire to sleep in a tree, either, but from where she sat, she could still see plenty of water. What if it was deeper than expected? Or full of debris they couldn't see? As Rachelle started to squirm around and dangle her feet off the branch, Lavender shouted, "Don't you think we should wait a little longer, Marisol? John?"

But John and Marisol were already climbing down.

With a deep sigh, Lavender surrendered and lowered herself out of the tree. The gravel was squishy under her feet, and a few flecks of muddy water sprayed up the sides of her legs as her feet hit the earth. She staggered in pain.

Lavender massaged her back near her tailbone and tried to shake the pins and needles from her legs. She was so stiff from sitting in frozen terror that she wasn't quite sure how she would manage to hike back to camp.

Marisol groaned as she stretched her arms, and John said, "Ouch."

"Don't be wimps. Once we get moving our muscles will loosen up," Rachelle told them.

Ha! She was one to talk about being a wimp. And why did Rachelle have to act like she had all the answers? But Lavender kept her thoughts to herself as the four made their way back toward the curve in the canyon, trying to return to the last place they'd seen their class.

They were mostly silent as they walked, trying to avoid puddles and branches and remnants of the flood. Lavender concentrated on her feet. One step. Then another. Veer to the right. Hop on the flat rock. Small jump to a bigger boulder.

Eyes glued to her path, Lavender rounded the bend. She heard the gasps before she saw it for herself. The sound filled her with dread.

Tearing her gaze from her sneakers, Lavender was suddenly face-to-face with a mountain of charred rubble. Rocks, boulders, branches, bushes, and even a few whole trees were clogging the narrow passage of the canyon. The flood had washed everything into the ravine and tons of debris had lodged in this slender, curved section of the canyon. It formed a natural barrier, sealing them off from the others. There would be no backtracking through the wash. No easy way to return to their class.

9

"Maybe we can climb over it," Rachelle said in a voice that reeked of doubt. She reached out and touched one of the logs. Her hand came away smeared with ash.

John studied her hand and then looked back at the barrier. "The storm must have hit somewhere that there was a wildfire," he said. "And everything got washed here."

"That's what I don't get," Marisol said. "It wasn't raining here. The sky was hardly even cloudy. How did we end up in the middle of a flash flood?"

Lavender said, "I remember a news story my mom told me. A bunch of people got caught in a flash flood way north of here, and when it hit, the sky where they were was totally blue. The actual rainstorm was really far away."

"What happened to them?" John asked.

Remembering the end of her mom's story, Lavender was quiet a long minute.

Marisol spoke for her. "They died, didn't they?"

"Some of them," Lavender said reluctantly.

"Well, thanks for sharing *that*," said Rachelle. "But guess what? We already survived." She started shifting some of the smaller branches. "We'll dig our way out of here with our bare hands if we have to."

"Rachelle! No!" John said.

He was too late. Water was already seeping from the debris Rachelle had moved. They all jumped back.

"Whoa," Marisol said. "What was that?"

"It's just water," said Rachelle.

"Just water that almost killed us a couple hours ago!" Lavender said.

"Let's not argue," said John again, his shoulders tense. "We don't know what's on the other side of all those branches. What if they're acting like a dam? A ton of water could be trapped behind there. I don't think we should move any of it."

Lavender waited for Rachelle to argue with John.

Rachelle always thought her ideas were good ones—no matter what anyone else had to say—but eventually, to Lavender's surprise, Rachelle nudged her toe into a fresh puddle where water had seeped out of the brambles and said, "Fine. You're probably right."

Marisol was studying the canyon. Lavender had seen that expression on Marisol's face before. It was the same look she got when they were doing math homework together and Marisol was trying to solve out a really difficult problem.

Now Marisol asked, "But if we don't go over the dam, how do we get out of here?"

Lavender could think of only one way, but Marisol didn't wait for a reply. "Help!" she cried out. She cupped her hands and shouted again at the top of her voice. "Help! We're down here! Someone help us!"

The only answer was Marisol's own voice echoing off the rock walls.

"Come on," Marisol said, sounding desperate. "The class can't be that far away. They wouldn't leave without us. Maybe they'll hear us."

A sliver of fear shot through Lavender. Until Marisol mentioned it, it had never occurred to

Lavender that the class could have left without them. The teachers wouldn't just abandon four of their students. Would they? No, definitely not. The rest of the sixth grade had to be nearby. She joined Marisol. So did Rachelle. The three of them yelled again and again . . . until John caught their attention, waving his arms in an urgent no-don't-do-that gesture.

"Careful," he hissed as the last echo of their voices died away. "You shouldn't do that."

"Why not?" Rachelle asked.

"You could start a rockslide."

"What are you talking about?" Rachelle said.

"Haven't you seen it in movies? It happens all the time."

"Those are just movies," said Lavender. "Scientifically, I don't think it's possible."

"I wouldn't bet on it," said John darkly. "After all, they told us rain and flooding are almost impossible this time of year."

"Good point," said Lavender. She'd been having astonishingly bad luck: getting ditched by Marisol; finding out that the telescope money was stolen; sitting on the bus with John, who didn't want to talk with her; and now she was stuck in a ravine after a flood tried to kill her . . . "I've been having some bad luck recently."

"No one is there anyway," Marisol said. "They would have answered by now if they could hear us."

"But they've gotta be waiting for us," John said. Then he ruined it, by adding, "Right?"

Lavender rubbed her arms and tried to think of the easiest way to rejoin their classmates. The dam was between them and the others. The ravine walls in this part of the wash were too steep to climb. Their only option was to walk until they found a place where they could hike out of the canyon. They couldn't just stay trapped here forever. So Lavender did what she did best. She took over.

"Then we walk that way," Lavender said, pointing back in the direction of the tree. "We need to go that way until we find a way out of the canyon."

"Then what?" John asked.

"We walk back along the canyon's ledge in the direction of our class. They'll be there, looking for us."

The other three exchanged looks.

"Fine," huffed Rachelle. "Let's just get this over with. I'm getting hungry, and you are pretty much the last people I want to be stranded in the wilderness with."

"Hey," Marisol said.

"You know that I'm not talking about you," Rachelle said. She marched away from the blockage, away from the last place they'd seen their teachers and friends. The wet sand and gravel squelched under their feet as they picked their way between puddles. Lavender tried not to wonder what the chances were that another flood would come or that the natural dam of leaves and branches and rocks would break. Would more water come roaring toward them, this time without any notice? She sped up her footsteps.

As the sun sank steadily lower on the horizon, the huge, distant clouds from earlier in the day broke into smaller puffballs. A slight breeze rustled its way through the slender branches of desert brush that dotted the canyon floor.

Rachelle complained that her new hiking shoes were being destroyed by all the muck left behind from the flood, and Marisol made a few sympathetic noises, but otherwise they walked in silence.

The poufy clouds on the mountainous horizon had turned different shades of pink and gold by the time they came to a section of the wash where the ravine walls were less severe. There was even a series of natural divots that Lavender thought looked like some sort of primitive path.

"What about here?" Lavender said, but there was an unexpected echo. Marisol had said the exact same thing at the exact same time. They must have both spotted the same crumbling, unmarked trail within milliseconds of each other.

"Whoa," John said, looking back and forth between them. "That was weird."

Lavender smiled. She and Marisol often had the same ideas: It had happened before. They could even finish each other's sentences. "Great minds . . ." Lavender said, hoping that Marisol would finish the phrase, but instead of saying "think alike," Marisol said, "So are we climbing out here or not?"

"Yes." Rachelle breezed past. "Get me out of this death trap. And I'm not going last this time!"

She started pulling herself up the sides of the steep slope. Lavender followed, ungracefully hopping from one boulder to another. At one point, Rachelle slipped, sending a spray of loose gravel trickling down behind her and falling into the wash. "Hey, watch it," Lavender yelled up at her.

Once she reached the last boulder and left the ravine behind forever, Lavender felt her worries melting away. Now they just had to follow the edge of the canyon. They would catch up to the rest of their class in no time. Everyone had survived the flood—and with a rush of warmth, Lavender remembered that was because of her. Thanks to her radio. Rachelle could never make fun of her "nerdy" hobbies ever again. Everyone would finish the hike—together—and when the entire class was back at camp, eating a warm meal around the fire, they would probably give Lavender a standing ovation. She would be the hero. Again.

She was going to be the most popular kid in class, way more popular than Rachelle. And once Marisol had time to realize that Lavender had risked her own life to save her, Marisol would apologize for abandoning Lavender. She and Marisol would be best friends like they were meant to be. Everything would be all right.

A sharp slapping sound grabbed Lavender's attention. She turned to see Marisol and Rachelle sharing a high five. Wanting to join in their celebration, Lavender shouted out, "We did it!" She held her two fists in the air over her head and smiled like she didn't have a care in the world. If her legs weren't sore and cramped from perching in the tree and climbing the canyon, she would have jumped up and down.

Her shout echoed off the rocks and repeated through the wilderness. It was returned with an answering cry, a faint, high wail. At first, Lavender thought it was human, probably someone from their class who was looking for the four of them. Then the noise sounded again, clearer this time: an eerie howl.

10

"Wh-what's that?" Marisol asked.

A hush followed. Then more howling. From every direction.

"Coyotes." John said it in a whisper, as if the animals might hear and attack. Another howl sounded—this one a loud, long cry that made shivers run up and down Lavender's arms.

"They sound really close." Rachelle shifted her weight from one foot to the other.

"Maybe they're looking for their pack," Marisol said. "Didn't Mr. Bob say something about coyotes sleeping in packs?"

"Like I paid attention to him," Rachelle said. "He talked forever."

"They could be looking for their pack," said John. "Or my dad said they hunt big prey in groups sometimes."

Lavender wished she'd listened more closely to Mr. Bob. Coyotes. What were you supposed to do when you were lost in the wilderness and surrounded by coyotes? Other than panic? Was this one of those throw-rocks-and-yell scenarios?

Rachelle's feet gritted against the dirt as she tensed. Something about her posture reminded Lavender of a runner about to get in position for a race.

"Hunting big prey? Like humans?" Marisol asked. She looked as nervous as Rachelle. Lavender had to fight back her instinct to hold Marisol's hand or give her a hug. After all, Marisol was afraid of dogs. A Rottweiler had bitten her when she was in first grade, and she'd had to get stitches. There was still a faint scar on her arm.

More howls echoed from every direction. They were surrounded. This time, the goose bumps weren't only on her arms; Lavender could feel the chills going the length of her spine.

"We have to get out of here," Marisol said. She danced a little in place.

John shook his head. "It's more dangerous to run. Remember what Mr. Bob said? They'll chase if you—"

He was cut off by a particularly loud howl, followed by a series of yips. At least one of the animals was closing in on them. Lavender almost expected to see it leaping through the air toward them.

"GO!" Rachelle's voice was so piercing that Lavender jumped about a foot in the air. Meanwhile, Rachelle pushed John aside, snagged Marisol's wrist, and sprinted away from the group. Without making a conscious decision, Lavender found she was running through the wilderness, too.

She could hear yips right behind her. Was a coyote following them? She put on an extra burst of speed. John was shouting something as he broke into a run with the rest of them. And then Lavender could hear only her own breath as she fought to pull enough oxygen into her lungs.

They did not run in a straight line. No, each time a new howl sounded, Rachelle would yank Marisol in a new direction, twisting and turning in an effort to get as far from the source of the sound as possible. Lavender thought her heart would pound out of her chest as she raced alongside them. She ran between pines and leapt over small rocks. Her arm scraped against some sort of yucca, but she ignored the stinging sensation as blind fear sent her zigzagging after Rachelle.

Lavender kept gasping for breath—her lungs empty of all air, her side a stabbing pain, and through the fog of panic, she finally registered what John was saying: "Stop! Stop!"

Rachelle and Marisol slowed and came to a rest. Lavender halted right behind them and leaned with one hand against a pine tree, taking great big gulping breaths.

"You shouldn't run from wild animals!" John was calling as he caught up to them. "They'll only chase you, and if you think you can outrun a coyote, you're living in a dream world."

"Whatever," said Rachelle. "It worked, didn't it? I don't hear the coyotes anymore, do you?"

Marisol shook her head. "Do you think we're safe? Do you think more are coming?"

Still panting and breathless, Lavender listened. No more howls. No sound of footsteps. As oxygen returned to her lungs and her mind cleared, Lavender straightened. She looked in every direction.

Not a single coyote in sight.

But no ravine, either.

They had left their only guidepost far behind them.

"Where are we?" she asked.

All three of the others snapped their attention to Lavender.

"Look around." Lavender swept her arm in a wide arc.

The others scanned the wilderness. Rocks. Pines. Cacti. Yucca. Rocks. Hills and mountains. Every direction the same. There was no path. No visible footprints. No landmarks. Without knowing the area, everything looked the same.

"We're lost," Marisol said in a flat voice.

Lavender nodded.

"No, no, no." Rachelle shook her head, in deep denial. "We can retrace our steps."

John snorted. "Good luck with that."

Marisol turned in a slow circle. "I don't think I even know which way we came from."

"It was that way." Rachelle pointed a random direction.

"I don't think so . . ." Marisol said.

"Or was it that way?" Rachelle's voice actually faltered.

"Face it," said Lavender. "You ran off, and now we're completely lost."

"You were running just as fast."

"What do we do now?" Marisol asked.

"John, try your phone again," Rachelle ordered. "We're not at the bottom of a wash anymore. Maybe you'll get a signal from here."

John pulled it out. Marisol and Rachelle clustered around him. They locked hands, and even in the wilderness, even now, Lavender's heart clenched at the sight.

John dialed 911. Still nothing. He tried again and again.

While he called repeatedly, Lavender fished out her radio. Not wanting to hear Rachelle's rude remarks if it failed again, Lavender walked away from the group. When she could still see the others but was certain she was out of hearing range, Lavender began scanning frequencies. She felt like doing a cartwheel when she paused on one and heard voices. This was it. They were saved.

"Mayday, Mayday," she transmitted.

"Thinking of using maple for the new cabinets," one of the disembodied voices crackled.

"This is an emergency! Come in," Lavender said into the radio.

"Maple is an awfully tricky wood to work with." Another voice came in more faintly than the first.

Why weren't these people responding to her distress signal? She could pick them up with her radio, but they didn't seem to hear her.

"Mayday! Mayday!" she called again into her radio.

"Well, I ain't gonna use any of that expensive curly maple if that's what you mean."

Lavender felt like her insides were being held between two clamps and twisted as she realized that they must be talking on a repeater. Without the settings for that repeater, her small handheld radio wouldn't be able to reach them. This was worse torture than being stuck in a tree with Rachelle during a freak flood.

Then a sudden hope surged through her. Hadn't her dad said something about a note? She'd been so distracted by her drama with Marisol that she hadn't really listened to her dad, but they had planned to talk while she was at camp. He'd had to have given her the settings for the repeater. Lavender began tearing through her backpack.

Empty bag of trail mix. Sunscreen. Water bottle. Toilet paper roll. But no note.

Had she heard her dad wrong? A memory flickered: Lavender suddenly recalled the stuff she'd dropped on the bus and forgotten about. The note that could save their lives was probably lying on the floor of their school bus. The thought made Lavender feel ill.

Discouraged beyond belief, Lavender jammed everything into her backpack and slowly returned to the others. She did not say anything to the others about the near-rescue. It would be cruel to taunt them with how close they'd come to getting help.

With every passing moment, the shadows were lengthening. Night was falling.

"It's no use," John was saying between clenched teeth. "I'll try again from a different place, but we're not getting through here, and I'm just wasting battery."

He powered down his phone.

Lavender took a deep breath and spoke in a hollow voice she hardly recognized. "We're not getting back. Not tonight."

11

"No, no, no, no." Rachelle shook her head and even stomped her feet. With each shout, John tensed. He looked ready to bolt. Not Lavender. She was holding in a smirk. Here were Rachelle's true colors. A babyish tantrum, compared to Lavender's own level-headed behavior. She waited for Marisol to draw away.

Instead, Marisol put an arm around Rachelle. "It's okay."

"You want to stay out here overnight?" Rachelle asked.

"No. Of course I don't want to," Marisol answered, glancing toward the gold horizon, where the sun had already disappeared behind the mountains, "but if we can find a safe shelter until tomorrow, don't you think we have a better chance in the daylight?"

Rachelle followed her gaze.

"Plus," Marisol said, "I remember my uncle saying you're more likely to be found if you stay in one place than if you go in circles."

"Good point," John said. He'd stopped backing away. "What if we look for shelter over there?" He pointed toward a clump of boulders.

"Anything that will protect us if those coyotes come back," Marisol said.

"No way," Rachelle said. "I am not sleeping in a bunch of rocks. It's probably full of snakes and spiders."

In her soul, Lavender agreed with Rachelle, but she would rather become a flat-earther than agree with Rachelle. So she said, "Good idea, John. Let's go."

Lavender marched toward the rocks, hoping that this time Rachelle would throw such a mega-tantrum that Marisol would stop trying to comfort her and tell her to bug off. And if Lavender got her friend back, then sleeping outside in the middle of nowhere with no dinner would almost be worth it.

≈

Nope. No way. Not worth it. Lavender completely changed her mind by the time she reached the boulders. She was not going to sleep between the rocks. Turned out, she would rather agree with Rachelle than crawl in *there*.

Lavender peered into the rocks. They were stacked on one another at the base of a small hill, and they formed a little nook—a pitch-black cave. A tiny dark tunnel that was probably full of killer bees or bats or scorpions or black widows or tarantulas or rattlesnakes or a thousand other creepy-crawly, potentially deadly things.

"Perfect," John said, studying the setup.

"Have you lost your mind?" Rachelle said. "Who knows what's in there?"

Lavender bit back a groan. She despised being on the same side as Rachelle.

"It's dry, and it'll be warmer than out here," John said.

"What if we miss the people looking for us because we're hiding in there?" Lavender asked. There. That was a valid point, and it wasn't the exact same objection as Rachelle's.

"What people?" John said.

"Search and rescue? Don't you think the teachers

will call 911 or something? Doesn't someone have to be looking for us?" Lavender heard her own voice get higher and higher pitched as she spoke. She was more worried than she was admitting to herself. She took a deep breath and tried to stuff down the looming panic.

"You're assuming they made it back," Rachelle answered. "For all we know, they're still walking in circles in the middle of the wilderness."

"And if anyone is looking yet," John said, "I bet it will be a long time before they extend the search this far. Think about it, they probably assume that we're near the wash."

"Or in it." Marisol said the words that Lavender didn't want to hear.

"You mean they'll think we . . . *drowned?*" she asked.

"Probably," John said. "It's what I'd think. You saw that flood. If they didn't see us get out, I bet they think we got caught in it."

Lavender's throat grew tight, and for a second, she thought she might burst into tears. What would her parents think? She took a few deep breaths. If John and Marisol were right, then that meant not only were they stuck sleeping alone in the wilderness overnight—it also meant that there would be no magical rescue. Any search would be for bodies, miles downstream. This wasn't just a waiting game. It meant that they had to save themselves.

But how?

"Well, that sucks," Rachelle said.

"Understatement of the century," Marisol said with a shaky laugh.

There was another silence. Lavender wanted to curl up in a ball and cry, but instead, she straightened her shoulders. In a way, this wasn't that different than the concert. Someone had to take over. Someone had to direct things. "Okay," she said. "So, shelter?"

"I still think the rocks could work," John said. "And I'll check for animals before we go in if Rachelle's worried about it."

"Seriously? We're actually going to sleep in there?" Rachelle wailed.

"What other option is there?" Marisol said.

The four walked over to the clump of boulders. Marisol squatted next to John at the entrance. Her voice sounded like she was forcing it to be upbeat. "How will you see?"

"I've got a flashlight," John said.

"You do?" Lavender asked. "Why didn't you say something sooner?"

John didn't answer. He was rummaging in his backpack. For the first time, Lavender really noticed how full his bag was. It was stuffed. She was again impressed with his tree-climbing skills. A moment later, John reemerged, flashlight in hand. He flicked it on.

"I wish we had a black light," Marisol said.

"What?" Rachelle asked. "Why?"

"To make the scorpions glow," Lavender answered without really thinking—she was still studying John's bag, but when she looked away, Marisol gave her a small smile. It felt like the first genuine sign of friendship that Marisol had shown since . . . well, since before the disastrous concert.

Lavender knew they were both remembering that summer in third grade when they hunted scorpions at the park with a black light almost every night. Marisol always won. Lavender hated scorpions. She'd only gone along with it because back then Marisol had wanted to be an entomologist and Lavender hadn't wanted anyone to know she was terrified of them. Of course, all of that was before Marisol started changing. But even if some things were different, you couldn't erase the kind of history that Lavender and Marisol shared—all the years of school lunches and field trips and sleepovers and birthday parties.

"This will have to be good enough," John said. He knelt in the dirt, and then, slowly, he crawled halfway into the nook between rocks.

"Be careful," Rachelle said.

"Don't worry. There's nothing in—" John broke off midsentence. "Aaarrggghhh! Get it away, get it away."

Screaming, he scrambled backward from the cave, tripped over Lavender's feet, and landed on his butt.

"What is it? There's a rattlesnake, isn't there?" Rachelle shrieked, dancing back.

Lavender wanted to be brave, but her feet wouldn't cooperate. She was inching away without meaning to.

"It's not a snake," John gasped. "There's some kind of—some kind of—"

"Some kind of what?" Marisol crouched and looked as tightly wound as the others—ready to sprint for safety at the first hint of a rattle.

"Bug." John finally got the last word out.

"Oh." The tension drained right out of Marisol. Big dogs, coyotes, and flash floods might give Marisol the jitters, but Lavender had never seen a bug that could faze her friend. "What kind?"

"How should I know?" John asked. "But it's the size of a house." John still hadn't moved from his spot near Lavender's feet.

"Do you think it's venomous?" Lavender asked him.

"Anything that big has to be dangerous."

"Oh, give me that." Marisol swiped the flashlight from John. "I'll check."

Lavender watched proudly. She and Marisol had become best friends during career week in second grade. They were the only two kids in the whole class who had wanted to be scientists. Though Lavender had never been particularly interested in biology. She was much more into physical sciences and things like astronomy or electronics.

Marisol wedged herself in the crevice between the rocks. They were silent, waiting to hear what she would say. John flinched when Marisol's voice finally echoed out from between the rocks.

"Wow! I've never seen one of these in real life before."

"What is it?" Lavender leaned over John, both curious and nervous. Lavender told herself that she wasn't scared of bugs; she just had a healthy respect for their personal space.

"It's a Jerusalem cricket." Marisol scooted out of the tiny cave, holding one palm flat. When she stood up and shone the flashlight on it, John started moving backward in a demented crabwalk and Rachelle gave a short, shrill scream.

Revolted, Lavender examined the creature on Marisol's open palm. John was wrong: The thing was smaller than a house. But it still was a good three or four inches long. And hideous. If a scorpion, a cricket, and a bumblebee had an alien baby with a human head, it would look exactly like the abomination Marisol held so calmly.

Lavender forced herself not to shriek or jump back. She wanted to prove herself to Marisol, who seemed to have momentarily forgotten that she was fighting with Lavender. So with her fingernails digging into her palms, Lavender said calmly, "Do you think we can eat it?"

Rachelle gave another little shriek, crying out, "You're disgusting!"

"What? They're a good source of protein. Haven't you ever seen Bear Grylls?" said Lavender. "I'm hungry—aren't you?"

"I'd have to be a lot hungrier to even think about eating that thing," Rachelle said.

"Don't worry," Marisol told the bug, shielding it from Lavender. "I won't let anyone eat you."

John snorted. "That thing can take care of itself." He was still crouched on the ground, giving both Marisol and the monster cricket the stink eye.

"Well," Marisol admitted, "I have heard they can bite pretty hard if you mess with them, but they're really good bugs. They're not poisonous. They eat dead things and help keep the land clean."

"Sick. That's just sick." Rachelle's eyes shut tight, and she shook her head. "Will you put that down somewhere so we can get on with it?"

Marisol shrugged and walked a few steps away from the others before coaxing the monster onto the ground near a little shrub. "Go on, little niña de la tierra," she said.

"Hurry up," Rachelle ordered. "It's getting cold out here."

12

Mrs. Henderson had warned them that the temperatures at night in the spring could drop into the forties or even the upper thirties. Before the trip, the teacher had checked that every student had an appropriate jacket or coat, but no one had thought to bring a coat on the hike—not in the middle of the day, when it was a sunny eighty degrees.

Well, no one except John.

As Marisol finished up with her demon bug, John reached into his backpack. He pulled out a black jacket and offered it to Rachelle. "I've got my hoodie, so you can wear this if you're cold," he said.

Lavender pictured her own coat, folded in her

duffel bag in the tent at camp. It had never occurred to her that she might not be back in time to wear it. Lavender expected Rachelle to thrust her arms into John's coat and claim it for the rest of the evening. But Rachelle did neither of those things.

"Wow, thanks," Rachelle said. "What else do you have in your backpack? It's almost like you were planning to spend the night out here."

"Not exactly," John said.

"Do you have anything else we can use?" Rachelle asked.

"What about food?" Lavender added, not wanting Rachelle to get first dibs on whatever else John might have in his bag. Shivering slightly, Lavender couldn't quite tear her eyes away from the coat. She wished Rachelle would just put it on already or offer it to her if she wasn't going to wear it.

"I've got enough protein bars for us each to have one," John answered.

"Why didn't you say so before?" said Rachelle. "I've been *starving* for hours."

John shrugged.

"Protein bars? Can I have one?" Marisol asked, rejoining the group.

"Let's wait a moment," said Rachelle. "If the cave

is bug-free, we can climb in the rocks, take turns sharing John's jacket, and eat dinner."

Lavender didn't know if she was impressed or annoyed. Rachelle was so bossy. Lavender hated that, but at least Rachelle wanted to share. That was the last thing Lavender had expected.

"I guess so," John said with another shrug. He took the flashlight back from Marisol and did a final sweep of the cave. "I don't see anything else in here."

"Did you check for black widows?" Rachelle said.

"I'll look," Marisol offered, and Lavender just knew that she was hoping to find a second Jerusalem cricket or some other equally exciting specimen.

"Thanks," said Rachelle. "If you don't mind, I'm going to sit down while you guys get the shelter set up. These shoes are really hurting my feet."

What did Rachelle expect? You didn't have to be an outdoor expert to know that hiking in brand-new shoes was a huge mistake.

Marisol's voice echoed from inside the rocks: "I've got something." And suddenly Lavender no longer wanted to be hanging out at the edge of the rocks . . . just in case some six-legged monstrosity made a bee-line for her. She would stand with Rachelle. No, behind Rachelle. Human bug shield.

But as she made her way over to Rachelle, Lavender couldn't believe her eyes. Even in the dim light of late evening, Lavender could clearly see what Rachelle was doing. She had taken off one shoe and was slowly dribbling her water over both her bare foot and the sneaker. She had a bundle of pine needles in one hand.

"You can't waste water like that!" Lavender snapped.

Rachelle paused and looked up. Caught red-handed. "It's not a waste."

"It is if you're using it cleaning your stupid new shoes."

"I'm cleaning my blister, too."

Rachelle had no respect for the desert. She hadn't lived in Arizona as long as Lavender. She didn't understand how important water was in a place where it was so scarce. Later, Lavender realized that if she'd just stayed calm and explained, things probably would have been all right. But as all the stress and fear of the day overwhelmed her, Lavender lost her last shred of patience.

"Stop wasting it." Lavender lunged for Rachelle's Hydro Flask.

Instinctively, Rachelle flinched and knocked over

her bottle. Half the water spilled to the ground before she could put it back upright. "Look what you made me do!"

"What *I* made you do? You're the one pouring our drinking water on the ground."

"It's not *our* drinking water; it's mine."

Marisol joined them, flashlight in hand. "All set." She paused, shining the light from Lavender to Rachelle to the spill. "Oh no! What happened?"

"Ask her." Rachelle pointed to Lavender.

"Rachelle spilled it," said Lavender. "I was trying to stop her from wasting it. She was cleaning her shoes or her feet or whatever with it."

"Because I don't want my blister to get infected."

"Drinking water is more important right now!" Lavender felt like crying. How could Rachelle be so blind to the obvious? Why couldn't Marisol see through her?

"It's my water," Rachelle said. "I can use it how I want to."

"Stop it! Both of you!" Marisol exploded in a voice that Lavender had never heard her use before. "You just spilled some of our only water, because you can't get along for more than two seconds. Do you know how pathetic that is?"

"Yes. About as pathetic as using drinking water to wash your feet when you're lost in the desert," Lavender said. She was right, Marisol would have to see that.

"That's not the point," Marisol said.

"Then what is?" Lavender crossed her arms.

"The point is that we're kind of in trouble here, and if you don't learn to just get along with Rachelle, we could all die!" Marisol threw her hands up in a disgusted gesture.

Me? Lavender wanted to shout right back that it wasn't her fault and that if they died in the middle of the wilderness, it would be because Rachelle led them in circles running from coyotes and wasted their precious water supply. The only thing that stopped Lavender from shouting it back was that . . . it actually was her fault.

All afternoon, she'd been trying to push down the thought. But here it was.

She'd lied. She'd tricked Rachelle and Marisol into a nonexistent game of sardines. And if any of them ran out of water or went hungry or was hurt or worse, the blame lay with only one person. Her.

13

Lavender made her way over to sit by John. It was almost completely dark now. The last glow of twilight was fading, and John's outfit blended into the rocks. As she drew closer, Lavender could see that he was huddled in his red hoodie outside their temporary shelter, sitting in a tight knot, knees drawn up to his chest. He looked as uncomfortable and depressed as Lavender felt.

"You okay?" she asked.

"No," he said.

"Oh," she said. "Me either."

In silence, he handed her a protein bar.

"Thanks," Lavender said, not bothering to wait until they were in the shelter. She ripped it open and took a small bite. Thrilled as she was to eat something—anything—she didn't enjoy it. The bars were dense and gritty and fake-tasting.

She picked at it for a few minutes until John said, "Even if you don't like it, you should try to eat. We all need the calories."

"Did you eat one?"

He held up an empty wrapper. "Just finished it."

Lavender grimaced, but she took another bite of the strawberry yogurt protein bar without comment. For a minute, there was only the sound of Lavender chewing, and then she heard a rustle as John pulled the hood over his head. He tugged it down so low that it looked like he wanted it to swallow his face. Was he just chilly, or was he trying to escape her company? It was hard not to take it personally.

"Am I bothering you?" Lavender asked. "Or is something else bugging you?"

"Bugging. Ha," he said in a muffled voice. "That's a good one."

"What? Oh, because of the Jerusalem cricket." Lavender didn't even attempt a pity laugh. She was too exhausted and too cold. With a tired sigh, she took another bite of the protein bar. "You've been acting weird all day."

Lavender waited. If anything, he should say something about being lost or hungry or scared of the coyotes. Other than Rachelle, those were the things upsetting Lavender.

Instead, out of nowhere, John answered, "I just really don't like fighting."

"What?"

"I wish you and Rachelle wouldn't argue so much."

Lavender straightened her back, offended. "*She* was fighting with me. Rachelle started it. She always starts it. Like just now, she was actually using her drinking water to clean a blister on her foot. She's lived here over a year now. Can you believe she was wasting water like that?"

Lavender paused, waiting for John to chime in, as full of indignation as she was, but when she glanced at him, his head was bent, and Lavender got the impression that he was staring determinedly at his feet.

So? She didn't get along with Rachelle. It wasn't a crime.

Their conversation was interrupted by a beam of light as Marisol and Rachelle materialized beside them.

"We found a good spot for a bathroom over there."

Marisol waved her hand toward a clump of bushes a few yards away. "Anyone want a turn with the flashlight before we go in the shelter?"

"I do," Lavender said. Marisol handed her the light, and Lavender grabbed the toilet paper from her backpack and went to squat behind the thick wall of branches. Away from the chatter of the others, Lavender started to feel very alone. She looked up to the night sky, where thousands of stars were shining. Normally, she would be thrilled to see so many, but just now, it made her feel very small and insignificant.

A branch near Lavender's right ankle shifted, causing her heart rate to double. Anything could be in the bushes with her. The litany of wild animals Mr. Bob had listed raced through Lavender's mind. She yanked her pants up and skittered back to the others, shivering from the temperature . . . and the terrible feeling that a rattlesnake was going to sink its fangs into her ankle at any second.

"Let's get in the shelter," she said, practically running up to the trio. "Being out here at night is giving me the creeps."

"After you." Rachelle gestured.

Of course, Rachelle wouldn't want to go in first, in

case there were any venomous spiders or scorpions they'd missed. But Lavender trusted Marisol completely. There wasn't a bug on the planet that would have escaped her attention.

Lavender crawled in, taking the flashlight with her, and the other three followed. Even with all four of them smashed together in the tiny space, there wasn't enough of John's jacket to go around. Still, it was better than nothing; the temperature was somewhat bearable with the body heat of four people in a small space. Lavender wasn't exactly warm . . . but she was less cold than before. And less scared. At least in here she felt in control of their surroundings.

The tiny cave was crowded, uncomfortable, and unnaturally quiet as Marisol and Rachelle ate their protein bars. Like they were afraid to talk about anything for fear of breaking into another fight.

As the others drifted off to sleep, Lavender stared at the ground and listened. She lived on a quiet street in the Phoenix suburbs. She was used to the sound of a distant dog barking, the thrum of passing cars, an occasional cricket, and the white noise of her ceiling fan.

She was not used to the sound of her classmates breathing and kicking and shifting around, and she was definitely not used to the sound of the mountains. Every breeze set off a cacophony of shifting branches, and every movement outside their cave set her heart racing. Chiricahua was home to bears, mountain lions, javelinas, coyotes, and a hundred other animals. As Lavender willed herself to fall asleep, she could not help but wonder what hungry creature might be lurking in the dark. More than once, she could have sworn she heard grunting and snuffling just outside their enclosure, which scared her until she decided that the sounds were probably Rachelle snoring.

In spite of the noise and fear, Lavender fell asleep at some point, because sometime later she jerked awake, shivering. It was still night when her eyes flew open, but less dark than before. The moon must have risen. A beam of milky light now filtered in through the opening of their little cavern. The light glinted off John's eyes, and Lavender realized that she was not the only one awake.

"Can't sleep?" he whispered.

"Too cold," Lavender answered, feeling around for the jacket. In her sleep, Marisol had tugged most of Lavender's portion off her. Lavender pulled a sleeve of the jacket over her lap, trying to take deep breaths and tell herself that she liked the cold. Her dad always insisted cold wasn't so bad if you embraced it rather than trying to fight it. It didn't help.

"I thought it might have been the coyotes," John said.

As she came more awake, the sound of howling caught Lavender's attention, and she wondered how she'd possibly been able to sleep before. There had to be dozens of the animals in the hills surrounding their temporary campout.

"Do you think they smell us?" Lavender asked.

"They won't mess with us," John said.

"How do you know?"

"My dad says wild animals don't usually try to eat humans unless they're starving. He used to take me and my brother camping all the time."

"Oh." Lavender tried to think of a better response. She had none. When you're cold, tired, hungry, thirsty, and lost in the wilderness in the middle of the night with your archnemesis and your former best friend, what is there to say to a boy you've known since first grade but never talked to much until now?

Lavender shifted. Her backpack was wedged between her shoulders and the rock behind her. At first she'd thought her book bag would provide a little cushioning, but now something was digging into her back, and it hurt. When she was done re-arranging herself, she looked over at John. He'd grown so still and quiet that she thought he'd gone to sleep again.

But John's eyes were wide open. Staring right at Lavender, he whispered, "I know what you did."

14

The blood in Lavender's veins turned to ice. Those words were even scarier than a flash flood crashing toward her. What could he possibly know? Every bad thing she'd ever done washed over her: the time in second grade when she'd borrowed a pencil from the art teacher and then just kept it, the time last year when she'd forgotten to do her history homework and told her teacher it was at home when it was really sitting incomplete in her backpack, the time she'd ripped a library book by accident and then put it back on the shelf without telling the librarian, the time she and Marisol had secretly streamed a movie on her mom's Netflix account that they had been told not to watch.

John was looking at Lavender like he knew all her worst secrets.

When she remained frozen and unable to answer, John leaned closer and whispered, "Why did you lie to them about playing sardines?"

Lavender gasped. "How did you find out?"

"When you used the bathroom, I asked them how they'd gotten separated from the group. And what they said didn't make sense. I was playing hacky sack with Jeffrey and Kyle, remember? I know they weren't playing sardines."

"Did you tell them there was no game?"

John shook his head and Lavender could breathe again.

He leaned forward a little. "Why did you lie?"

Lavender partly wanted to deny it, to make something up. But she was already guilty enough. And maybe if John understood, he wouldn't rat her out to Rachelle and Marisol. From many years of slumber parties, Lavender knew that Marisol was a heavy sleeper, but Lavender glanced over at Rachelle to make sure she was still asleep before admitting, "I was mad."

"About what?"

"Marisol is my best friend." She couldn't believe

she was telling him this. "She has been since we were eight years old, and now she just . . . started ignoring me. I wanted things to go back to the way they were."

"Sometimes things can't go back to the way they were," John said in a hollow voice that sounded about a hundred years old.

If she'd known him better, Lavender might have asked him what things. He sounded like he knew how she felt. John hadn't been sitting with Jeffrey and Kyle on the bus. By now, Lavender was almost positive he was dealing with the same kind of friend trouble that she had. Lavender felt tears stinging the backs of her eyes and was grateful for the darkness.

"I guess I don't get it," John said. She could see him shake his head. "How would tricking them fix anything?"

"I thought if I got Rachelle out of the way, I could just hang out with Marisol for a little while. And we could just be friends like we normally are and . . ." She paused. She almost didn't confess it, but then the words spilled out. "And I wanted to punish Rachelle. She's always butting in and Miss Popular and so bossy. I thought it would be funny to see her embarrassed when she realized that no one was looking for her. She'd probably throw a big tantrum, and Marisol would see what a drama queen she is."

John gave a soft low whistle. "Wow. That's mean."

"I'm not the mean one. Rachelle is," Lavender said with a sinking feeling in the pit of her stomach. "It's not like I knew a flood was coming. I never would have done it if I'd known it would be so dangerous."

"That doesn't make it less mean."

"But you know how Rachelle is, right?" Lavender said. "She gives people rude nicknames and talks behind their backs. She makes fun of people who don't think the same as her. You know she deserves a taste of her own medicine sometimes," Lavender said, wishing she could forget her own role in all that had happened.

"Lying about a game of sardines to embarrass someone else doesn't make you much better than she is."

Lavender felt her mouth drop open. She couldn't believe what he was saying. "Seriously? Is that what you think of me? You don't even know me."

John held up his hand. In the faint moonlight, she could see him gesturing between the four of them. "Maybe none of us really know each other."

"I know Marisol," Lavender said.

"Then why would she rather hang out with Rachelle than you?"

He might as well have punched her in the teeth. Lavender took a few deep breaths and reminded herself that it didn't really matter what John thought. The only things that really mattered were getting out of the wilderness alive and fixing her friendship with Marisol.

"Look," Lavender said after a long silence, "just promise that you won't tell Marisol and Rachelle, but especially Marisol, about the sardines thing."

"You want me to lie?"

She shook her head. "Yes. No. I don't know. Just . . . don't bring it up. They don't have to know that we got stranded because I tricked them. I do feel really bad about it now. But I didn't do it on purpose, and I'm really sorry you wound up lost with us. It's just—"

"Just what?"

"If you tell, it'll be even harder for us to get along," she said, remembering their earlier conversation. "It'll just be one more reason for us to fight."

"I won't tell," John said in a flat voice.

"Thank you," Lavender said. He didn't answer, and after a minute, Lavender wondered if he'd fallen asleep. She rubbed her arms, trying to warm them.

"Hey, John," she called in the same soft voice as before.

"What?" he answered.

"Why does it bother you so much? So what if we argue with each other?"

He was silent. She'd just about given up on an answer when John's muffled voice said, "It reminds me of my parents." He wouldn't answer any more of her questions, though, and she dozed off still waiting.

15

Lavender woke with the dawn and rubbed her eyes. They were glued shut from sleep and sandy grit. Blinking a few more times, she looked around the little nook. Marisol was still sleeping, curled under John's jacket, but neither Rachelle nor John was anywhere to be seen.

She was cold, stiff, thirsty, tired, and her face felt like it had been smashed into a rock all night . . . probably because it was. As Lavender straightened into a sitting position, she ran her fingers against her cheek and felt the indents the uneven surface had left on her skin.

But they had survived. Lavender had even slept in fits and starts. And John wasn't going to tattle on her. The four of them could figure out how to get back to camp. Or surely, by now search and rescue workers were looking for them. They would be out of the wilderness by lunchtime . . . and they would have a really good story to tell.

Feeling optimistic about the day ahead, Lavender promised herself that she wasn't a mean or bad person. And she would prove it to John by getting along with Rachelle. It would probably make Marisol happy, too. Lavender knew it wouldn't be easy, but she could do it.

Moving as quietly as possible, Lavender emerged from the shelter only to walk straight into Rachelle. She was standing two inches from the shelter. Her hands were on her hips, and she was scowling. Lavender had a sinking feeling that Rachelle had been waiting for her.

"I heard every word you and John said last night," she said.

Glancing around for an escape route, Lavender saw John wandering toward them from the direction of their temporary bathroom. Lavender wanted to yell helpful directions at him, something like "Red alert" or "Change course!" But that might wake Marisol, and Lavender did not want her to overhear this conversation.

"What are you talking about?" Lavender asked.

"Don't act like you don't know. I heard." She glared at John, who had paused a foot or two away from them, and then Rachelle pointed a finger at Lavender and poked her in the chest. "This is all your fault. You lied. You were trying to make me look stupid, and that's why we're stranded out here."

Lavender tried to swallow, but her mouth was dry and her throat tight. She had to make this go away before Marisol heard them.

"I—I'm sorry."

"Lavender's not the one who took the wrong turn on the hike. That was the teachers," John said quietly. Lavender glanced over at him. He looked like he wished he was back in the bushes, but he held his ground.

"Sure, take her side," Rachelle said. "At least we would be with the rest of our class if it wasn't for her."

"Maybe, but don't forget she saved them all in the first place," John said. "And then she went back to save you."

Lavender wanted to throw her arms around John and thank him. But she had to wonder why he was sticking up for her. Was he just trying to prevent another fight? Or was it because they were starting to be friends? Lavender didn't think that John shared his deepest thoughts with many people. Maybe it meant something that he'd told her about his parents.

"Rrrggghhh," said Rachelle. She threw her hands up in the air. "Why are you defending her? Why can't anyone else see through Lavender? She's a two-faced little liar who—"

"I really am sorry," Lavender interrupted, the knot of guilt curdling in her stomach. "I shouldn't have lied about sardines. It was stupid. I didn't know a flood was coming, or I never would have done it. Just please, please, please don't tell Marisol." Not now. Not when they were in the middle of the crisis. After they were rescued, after their fight was over, Lavender could tell her then. But not now.

"Are you guys talking about me?" Marisol's sleepy voice drifted out from inside the rock shelter.

"We're just trying to decide what to do next," Lavender called.

"Doesn't John's phone work yet?" Marisol asked, poking a rumpled head out from the between the rocks.

He shook his head. "I didn't have service here last night. It's not like it will be any different this morning."

"Brrr, it's cold." Marisol jumped up and down a couple of times as she pulled herself out of the cave, swathed in John's jacket. "Shouldn't you just check the phone once to be sure?"

"I guess," he said.

Lavender let out a breath she hadn't known she was holding. Rachelle hadn't said anything. With her fingers crossed behind her back, Lavender made a silent wish that it would stay that way.

While the others were busy with the cell phone, Lavender decided to try her radio once again. There was always the chance that there were new hikers or campers in the area who would have a radio with them. Plenty of outdoorsy, adventurer types used ham radios. And if there was someone like that in range, she wouldn't have to worry about the repeater settings. She would be able to talk to them directly.

Lavender turned her radio on and scanned through channels.

On one frequency, she got a promising change in static. Not wanting to disappoint her group, she didn't announce anything, but she leapt to her feet and started walking around, trying to warm up, but even more importantly, hoping to get to a position where her antenna could reach farther.

She pushed the button. Her heart raced.

"This is KG7XAB," she said, using her specially designated call sign. All licensed radio operators had one. It was sort of like a telephone number or Twitter handle.

Lavender let go of the transmit button and waited for a reply.

There was none. She tried again.

"This is KG7XAB. Come in, come in. Please come in. This is an emergency."

She could hear faint words! Something about their rigs.

"This is KG7XAB! We have an emergency!" she shouted.

No answer.

This was exactly the same thing that had happened before. It was agony. She could hear them, but they couldn't hear her. If only she knew how to talk with the repeater.

"Come in, come in," she cried into the radio. "Mayday, Mayday."

But no one responded to her distress call. After

a moment, the voices cracked and disappeared completely. She sank down on the ground, leaning against a rock.

A shadow fell across her, and Lavender looked up to see Rachelle looming above her.

"If John and Marisol can't get a signal on his phone, what makes you think your little radio could do anything?"

Several answers flitted through Lavender's mind. She could give Rachelle a long and detailed answer explaining how cell phones worked versus how radios worked. They were two totally different pieces of technology. But what was the point? Lavender was too distraught to form a coherent answer, and Rachelle didn't actually want to know. She only wanted to put Lavender down.

"What do you want?" Lavender said in a dull, flat voice, wishing she hadn't even attempted to use her radio. For a second, she'd been so sure that they were rescued.

"I want you to admit you were wrong, for one."

"I already apologized."

"And I want you to agree with me when I tell John and Marisol that we're going *my* way today." She pointed toward a mountain.

"Why? What do you think is over there?"

"I thought about it all night, and I'm sure that's the same mountain I was looking at from camp."

"No way. We should stay around here or try to find the canyon again. If we walk straight into the mountains and you're wrong, we'll end up even more lost than we are now."

"Ugh, you always think I'm wrong, but I know for a fact that if we go up there, we'll be able to see Mr. Bob's ugly RV and the rest of the campsite."

"How do you know?" Lavender asked. "There were mountains all around us."

Rachelle ignored her. "Maybe you don't know this about me, but I like to do things. I'm not the kind of person to sit around and wait for something to happen. I make things happen."

"But—"

"Like yesterday, if it was up to you, we would have sat in that tree all night. We'd still be in the wash."

Now Lavender was getting angry. How dare Rachelle make Lavender sound like she didn't get things done. Lavender wasn't the type to sit around, either. "Oh, yeah? Well, did you ever think—"

Rachelle didn't let Lavender finish the thought.

"Either we go my way, or I'm telling Marisol what you did."

Lavender blinked up at Rachelle in surprise. "Are you serious? You're going to blackmail me?"

"Marisol will never talk to you again if she finds out that you lied to her."

Rachelle and Lavender stared at each other in silence.

Marisol's voice cut through the stalemate. "Shoot!"

"No luck?" Rachelle called over to her.

"None," Marisol said as she and John joined them. "Now what?"

"I've been thinking it over, and I say we go that way." Rachelle pointed toward the mountain that she was so confident was one of the mountains they'd seen from their campsite.

"Why that way?" Marisol asked.

"It's in the direction of the campground, I'm sure of it."

"What makes you think so?" asked John.

At the same time, Marisol said, "I don't know. Maybe we should just stay here."

That's what Lavender had suggested! She held her breath, hoping that Marisol would be able to talk Rachelle into a different plan. The surrounding hills and rocks and mountains all looked the same. There was no way that Rachelle could actually know the right direction.

"I can't believe you want to just sit here and do nothing," Rachelle was saying to Marisol.

"Seriously, I'm sure that's what my uncle told me one time. I remember him saying that whenever people get lost, they always find the cars or plane wreckage or whatever first before they find the people. I think it might be better if we stop moving around."

"That sounds right," said John. "But we don't have any wreckage to attract attention."

"So you agree with me? We should keep walking," Rachelle said. It wasn't a question.

"I think," John said, "we should just have a good reason for going a certain way."

"I've got good reasons," Rachelle said. "One, like I already said, I'm sure that's the direction of our campsite. Two, I'll bet you've got a better chance of getting a phone signal from up on the mountain. Three, where are we most likely to find a hiking trail? On a mountain. If we go that way, it's only a matter of time until we're saved. And I'd rather rescue myself than just sit here and hope that someone finds us."

Lavender raised her eyebrows. Maybe Rachelle hadn't been exaggerating when she said that she'd thought about it all night. Lavender was almost convinced.

"What do you think, Lavender?" Rachelle spoke in a tone that was somehow syrupy sweet and venomous at the same time. Fear, like an electrical current, zapped through Lavender. Marisol had just started looking her in the eye and talking to her almost normally again. She couldn't let Rachelle ruin that now.

Lavender jumped to her feet. "Just that it's definitely safer to stick together and Rachelle does have some good points."

"Fine," said Marisol, "but can we at least do an inventory of our supplies first? I'm hungry, and I'd like to know everything we have before we just start walking up a mountain."

They did the inventory. It did not take long. There was no food.

16

They each had a partially drunk water bottle. Rachelle's was lowest at only a quarter full.

"We better drink it slowly," John commented.

Lavender nodded in agreement.

Rachelle uncapped her bottle and took a swig.

"What else is in your bags?" Marisol asked quickly.

They had Lavender's radio and John's cell phone. Lavender showed them her bottle of sunscreen, roll of toilet paper, and empty bag of trail mix. Lavender once again remembered the items that had fallen out of her bag on the bus—the paper, the hair ties, the granola bar. She wished she still had the granola bar now, but even more, she wished she had that paper!

"I can't believe that's all you brought," Rachelle snapped.

"Mrs. Henderson said to keep the bags light," Lavender snapped back. Her mom had sent her with enough snacks to last a month, but they were heavy, so she'd left all but the trail mix in one of the food storage bins. Yet another mistake in an unending list of unfortunate decisions.

John barely paid attention to the inventory of Lavender's bag. He'd acted all twitchy and then refused to let them touch his backpack.

"What are you hiding in there?" Lavender asked John.

"Nothing," he said.

"Who cares?" Rachelle said. "If we can't eat it, it doesn't matter. Let's get going. I want to be back to camp in time for lunch."

Lavender snorted. "That's about as likely as finding a cure for cancer while we're out here."

"Don't joke about that," Rachelle said in a sharp voice.

"Focus," Marisol said, planting herself between the two of them. "If John is sure he doesn't have food in his backpack, there's no time to lose."

"I don't have anything else in here," he said

quickly, jamming the flashlight back in his bag. Not the jacket. Marisol had passed it to Rachelle. They were all taking turns wearing it in the chilly early-morning air.

"Let's look for berries or some kind of fruit or seeds that we can eat," Marisol said. "I'm hungry."

"Sure," said John. "Because the desert is just full of berries and fruit."

"It is, too," Marisol said. "And this is more than just a desert anyway. It's like desert and forest and grasslands all combined. Look around."

"Can we just get going already?" Rachelle said.

As they walked, Lavender scanned the plants around them, half hoping she would stumble into a miracle: an apple tree or a peach tree. Before the trip, Mrs. Henderson had told them that the original ranchers out here had planted those. But even if they did find a fruit tree, it was probably the wrong season to harvest any of it. She might as well wish for a cheeseburger tree and a french fry bush.

And after a while, she forgot completely about the food. It wasn't the gnawing in her empty stomach that bothered Lavender. It was the thirst. Water, Lavender decided, was going to kill you one way or another. Just yesterday, they almost died in a freak flash flood. Now they were lost and wandering through the Chiricahua Wilderness with empty stomachs and mostly empty water bottles. A person could live weeks without food, but only a couple days without water.

She tried to ration the small sips from her water bottle as they walked—they weren't on the side of the mountain yet, but they were definitely in the foothills, and the landscape was gradually changing. They had left much of the cactus behind. There were more grasses, and more of the twisty bushes with bright red bark. The trees were thicker, too. Arizona could be like that. Even small elevation changes could completely transform the scenery.

They'd been walking for about an hour when Marisol fell back from Rachelle to join Lavender. It made her want to do a little happy jig. She refrained, in part because she was so tired she thought her legs might give out if she tried to jig.

"I'm getting worried," Marisol said.

"Me too," said Lavender, torn between being miserable that they were missing and thrilled that Marisol was talking to her like normal, like they'd never had a fight.

"My mom is always watching these detective

shows that say most missing people are found within twenty-four hours, and if they aren't . . ."

"Then what?"

"Every hour that goes by makes it less likely their families will ever see them again."

Lavender blinked rapidly. She cleared her throat a few times, telling herself that she *would* see her parents again. She just had to think rationally.

If Marisol was right, that meant they had fewer than twelve hours until their first twenty-four were up . . . and even less time than that until they were completely out of water. With every passing second, their situation was becoming grimmer. "Marisol," Lavender said, "how much do you have left in your Nalgene?"

Marisol shook it. "It's getting low. I've been trying not to drink it too fast, but my stomach is so empty, I think I'm drinking even more than usual."

Lavender paused. "Maybe we should try to find water."

Marisol stopped beside her. "I have an idea about that," she said eagerly. "But it'll probably take a while, so Rachelle won't listen to me. She's so sure we can get back to camp if we just keep walking."

"She's only doing that because it was her idea," Lavender said. "She's always in love with her own ideas."

"Gee, I wonder who else gets like that," Marisol said.

Lavender felt like she'd just walked into a brick wall. "What? Are you saying that Rachelle and I—"

"Were you saying something about water?" John interrupted, coming up from behind them.

"Sort of. I think we could get moisture from a cactus," Marisol said.

Lavender wanted to go back to whatever Marisol had been implying. Was she really comparing Lavender and Rachelle? But with a shake of her head, she decided to ask about it later. Not in front of John.

"You want to cut a cactus open for water?" he was asking. "Like in the movies? My dad said that doesn't actually work in real life."

"No," Marisol said, "I've been thinking how we can eat it. I didn't suggest it at first, because it'll be tricky, but I'm starving and dying of thirst, and they're really moist."

"Are you sure it's edible?" John asked.

"I've had it before," Marisol said.

"Do you mean, like, cactus fruit?" Lavender asked. Her mom had bought jelly made from cactus fruit a couple of times, and once her family had taken prickly pear candy as a gift to relatives who lived in Oregon.

Marisol shook her head. "No, I don't think the fruit is ripe now, but if we find a prickly pear, I've eaten the cactus pads before. My grandma cooks with them sometimes."

Before Lavender and John could agree or disagree, they were interrupted by loud footsteps as Rachelle charged toward them like an angry rhinoceros. "What is taking you guys so long? We don't have time to waste just standing around," Rachelle said. "I am not spending another night with coyotes and pigs—"

"Javelinas," Lavender corrected automatically. "You're thinking of the wild pigs Mr. Bob told us about."

"What makes you think I was talking about the javelinas and not you?" Rachelle retorted.

Lavender watched Marisol's mouth drop open. She actually looked shocked. It was like Marisol had forgotten that Rachelle was rude and bossy and awful. With a surge of glee, Lavender realized that Rachelle's real self was starting to show.

John's eyes were flicking between Lavender and Rachelle as if afraid another full-blown argument was going to break out. To Lavender, he sounded nervous as he said, "But Marisol had a good idea for breakfast. It would give us more energy to climb the mountain."

The stubborn rhinoceros expression disappeared, and Rachelle's face brightened. "Breakfast?"

"I tried explaining before," Marisol said.

Rachelle groaned. "Are you still talking about the cactus?"

"Well, I think it's a good idea," Lavender said.

"Me too," John chimed in.

"Please?" Marisol said.

"Ugh, fine," said Rachelle. "Let's make it quick. I don't want to be stranded out here overnight again."

"Okay, here's what we're going to do," Lavender said loudly. "I'm getting tired, and I'm sure we could all use a rest, so let's just look around here and as soon as we find a prickly pear, we can sit down and eat. Marisol, you look over there. John, you go over there. Rachelle, you take that direction." Lavender pointed them all in different directions. "I'll go down by those bushes." She nodded toward a clump of overgrowth—bushes and trees grew in a thick line directly to their south.

"I don't really get why we should split up," John said. "What if we—"

Lavender interrupted, "We'll find one faster this way."

"I don't want to argue with you, but maybe you shouldn't walk into—"

"Don't worry. I know what I'm doing." Lavender waved him off. She wasn't sure what John was worried about. Snakes, probably. But Lavender clearly remembered reading that water could often be found where plants, especially trees, grew more densely. She didn't want to get their hopes up, but forget about prickly pear—Lavender was already picturing herself shouting triumphantly, "Water! I found water!" They would come running, and even Rachelle would have to admit that Lavender had saved their butts again.

Lavender marched straight toward the dense shrubs. With every step, she grew more confident that she could find a stream hidden in the thick foliage. That would be even better. Plants grew in dense clumps along the temporary creeks and seasonal streams that sprang up after heavy rain. Given that there was a flash flood only yesterday,

Lavender felt she had good reason to hope she would find running water.

They needed it to survive, especially in a place as dry as Arizona.

As she approached the line of trees, Lavender heard a rustle. She stopped, turned, and saw her friends spread out in their different directions. Could the noise have come from one of them?

She took a few more steps.

The rustling grew louder.

Nope, not one of her friends.

There was definitely something in the bushes.

Lavender froze.

A twig snapped.

Maybe there were birds roosting in the scrub. Or squirrels. It was probably some small, defenseless creature, Lavender reassured herself. The scary things with big teeth belonged to the night. Didn't they? After all, they'd heard the coyotes and javelinas and those things at dusk and dawn and in the night.

The noise stopped.

She saw a lizard hop onto a rock and scurry away.

Lavender let out a breath. She'd almost had a panic attack over a harmless little lizard. Her backyard was full of them. No big deal. She took a few more steps toward the bushes.

She was safe from the wild things. The day was growing bright. It would be sunny . . . too sunny, if the warm feeling on Lavender's nose and back of her neck could be trusted. In all of yesterday's excitement, she had forgotten to reapply sunscreen. She would put more on before they started hiking up the mountain.

Picking up her pace, Lavender resumed walking toward the line of trees.

An entire bush shook and rattled.

She stopped.

This was no lizard or squirrel. It was bigger. Definitely bigger. Maybe it was a the coatimundi, one of the raccoon-looking creatures Mr. Bob said inhabited Chiricahua. Only, unlike raccoons, he said they were more active in the daytime.

But no. The thing that crawled out of the branches was a very different animal. Much bigger than any coatimundi or coyote. Mr. Bob had warned the class about these, but Lavender had never in her wildest dreams expected to walk into one.

She called a quiet warning to the others.

"Bear!"

17

Her strangled whisper caught in her throat. She could barely hear her own voice.

"Bear!" she tried again.

The words were quiet and harsh.

Lavender took a step back, almost tripping over a rock as the bear emerged the rest of the way from the bush. She heard a weird little whimper coming from her throat. Her arms were crossed over her chest, her hands clutching her neck like a choking person, which was strangely appropriate. Lavender felt like she was choking. The pulse in her neck pounded so hard, she thought it might explode.

Cartoon bears and teddy bears and caged bears

at the zoo . . . none of these did justice to the creature in front of Lavender. "Black bears are small," Mr. Bob had reassured the class when they first arrived at camp. Well, Mr. Bob was a noodle head. What did he know?

The monster in front of her looked like it could swallow Lavender's entire face in one bite. It had claws and teeth, and Lavender was not about to fight back no matter what Mr. Bob had recommended. His words parroted through Lavender's mind in a cruel parody of reality. At camp, surrounded by friends and teachers, she'd almost thought it was funny when he told them: "If you keep your campsite clean and lock up your food, you are not likely to see a bear. If one does attack, do not play dead and do not run. They will chase. We have black bears here, and the best way to deal with a black bear is to scare it off. Use bear spray; make yourself look bigger. If attacked, fight. But for the most part, black bears are not aggressive."

Too bad this bear had missed the memo about not being aggressive. Too bad Lavender didn't have any bear spray. Too bad she didn't have a secure location like a car conveniently nearby.

Maybe there were cubs around. That would

explain why the bear was rising to its rear legs. If Lavender thought the bear seemed large before, that was nothing compared to how it looked now. The bear towered over Lavender and made a deep huffing noise, snapping its teeth and rumbling, low and loud.

"It's a bear!" Lavender finally found her voice, shrieking loud enough for her friends to hear. John, Marisol, and Rachelle gasped as they finally noticed that Lavender was about to become a midmorning snack.

The bear, still snorting and growling, took a step toward Lavender. She wanted to run. All her instincts told her to run. With every molecule and every atom that made her Lavender Hypatia Blue-Morris, she wanted to run. She wanted to sprint. She wanted to fly out of there. She didn't care if Mr. Bob had said that she wouldn't be able to outrun a bear; she wanted to try.

Only she couldn't.

Lavender's brain was no longer in control of her legs. They simply would not listen. She felt as if the force of gravity had suddenly quadrupled around her. Lavender didn't have enough strength in her entire body to lift a single toe, never mind run.

The bear was not having any similar issues with gravity. It took a step toward her.

"Lavender, do something!" Rachelle shrieked.

Like what? For once, Lavender was open to suggestions . . . even if they came from Rachelle.

Too frightened to look away from the animal, Lavender could hear her friends' feet shuffling through the brush. Were they backing away? Abandoning her?

The bear, which had been briefly distracted by the sound of her friends, now refocused on Lavender, making more of the rumbling, huffing noises. The bear went down on its front legs again and started charging straight at her.

Lavender heard herself start whimpering again. She shut her eyes and braced herself for the attack, hoping that when she felt the first claw she would be able to move again. If she was going to go down, she wanted to go down fighting. She wondered what it would feel like when its paw swiped her skin. Lavender liked her skin how it was: whole and unshredded. She tried not to the think about the pain when those teeth and claws ripped into her.

A warm, foul huff hit her face. She knew if she opened her eyes, she would be only centimeters away from those razor-sharp teeth. Lavender squeezed her eyes more tightly shut. This was how her life ended. She never imagined it would be so gruesome. Or so smelly. Or so soon.

"Go away!"

"Get out of here!"

"Shoo, bear. Shoo!"

A chorus of shouts startled Lavender into opening her eyes. The noise must have startled the bear, too, because the hot, stinky breath disappeared from her face as the animal drew back from her. Suddenly it charged around Lavender and ran at the others. She spun around in time to see the bear heading for John, Marisol, and Rachelle. They were spread out in a semicircle, a few feet from one another, shouting and yelling. Rachelle held John's jacket above her head, and she shook it. John was waving around his red hoodie. Marisol was simply waving her arms.

"Watch out!" Lavender called.

Rachelle fell back a couple of steps as the bear bore down on them.

"No!" said John. "Hold your ground. It'll chase if you run."

Rachelle stopped yelling, but she kept the jacket

above her head, looking as tall as possible. For a heartbeat, Lavender thought Rachelle was going to be the one who wound up as bear food.

But John started jumping up and down.

"Yo, bear, over here! Leave her alone!" John waved his hoodie.

The bear stopped, switched directions, and ran a few steps at John.

"Stop it, bear! Don't bother him." Now Marisol shouted, distracting the bear from John.

The bear looked toward Marisol.

Rachelle found her voice again. "Go away." She repeated the words again and again. Lavender watched as they worked seamlessly to call at the bear and distract it over and over.

A knot eased in her chest, and she found herself able to speak.

"Get out of here, bear! Shoo!" Lavender screamed.

Maybe Mr. Bob knew something after all. The yelling and intimidation seemed to work. Without any warning, the black bear suddenly dodged past Rachelle and ran a little way downhill before it threw its paws around a trunk and started climbing a tree with a speed and skill that astonished Lavender.

The four of them stood, watching.

Marisol broke the shocked silence: "You guys, we did it."

Lavender's legs gave out. She collapsed in a heap in the dirt.

And just when she thought she could not be any more shocked by a turn of events, Rachelle was first to dash to Lavender's side.

"Are you okay?" Rachelle asked, grabbing Lavender by the cheeks and looking in her eyes.

Lavender tried to nod, which was difficult with Rachelle's death grip on her cheeks. "I think so. Are you?" Lavender managed to ask.

Rachelle let go of Lavender with a nervous chuckle. "I doubt I'll ever be okay again after this field trip."

"No kidding?" Lavender heard herself laugh back. "I think we got the science campout from the bad place."

"Is everyone all right?" Marisol flung herself at the two of them, giving Rachelle and Lavender no choice but to join her in a group hug.

John reached them next, still glancing over his shoulder toward the tree the bear had climbed. "That was awesome!" he said. "But I really think we should—"

Marisol interrupted him, leaping up to give him a quick hug, too.

"John, you saved us," she said. Marisol looked at Lavender, who was still on the ground next to Rachelle. "You were probably too distracted by the bear to hear him, but it was his idea to make ourselves look bigger and try to scare it, and it worked. Can you believe it? We actually worked together to scare off a bear? We did that. We scared off a bear."

"Everyone helped," John said with a quick smile, before looking over at the bear tree. "Don't you guys think we should keep moving? Before it comes back down."

Lavender nodded. As shaken as she was, Lavender still wanted to put as much distance between them and the bear as humanly possible.

"What about finding cactus?" Marisol asked.

"Right this second, I'd say getting away from that bear is more important," John said.

"Good point," Marisol said.

Rachelle stood and offered Lavender a hand. Lavender took it.

"Let's hurry," John said.

No one was going to argue with that. Together, the four began walking uphill toward the mountain, as fast and far away from the black bear as their legs could carry them.

18

As they hurried away from the bear, John sounded like his old self. He was jumping around and gesturing, and his voice was full of expression. "Did you see those teeth?" he asked. "They were huge!"

"The better to eat you with," Rachelle said.

Marisol laughed and said, "I think John was more scared of the bug than the bear."

It was fine for the others to joke, but Lavender didn't feel up to it. She could still feel the gust of hot air and smell the stench of rotten meat from its breath.

"And its eyes . . ." John ignored their teasing about the night before. "I could see the red lines, like, all those blood vessels."

"He's not a monster," said Marisol.

"You can say that," Lavender said, "because it didn't almost eat your face. It looked like a monster to me."

"I thought he was actually really cute," Marisol said. "And it's not the bear's fault we were in his space. He was here first."

"When did we even decide the bear was a he?" Rachelle asked.

"Right?" Lavender said. "I thought it might be a she. Maybe she was so aggressive because there were cubs nearby."

"Yeah," said Rachelle, "and we accidentally got between her and her babies."

"If there were babies, I wish we could have seen them. I bet they're adorable," Marisol said.

John snorted. "We're lucky we didn't see the cubs. If we'd gotten that close, we'd be dead."

Lavender put a hand on the trunk of a pine tree. It trembled. They hadn't been walking for that long. She would have guessed that they'd gone maybe twenty minutes or so, but they had gone fast enough that she was sure there was a good distance between them and the bear. Either way, Lavender was still shaky and maybe in shock. "We've got to be pretty far from the bear now. How about a break, guys?"

"I could use a short rest," Rachelle agreed. Lavender did a double take. Being on the same page with Rachelle was almost as scary as the bear attack.

Marisol and John also stopped, but John refused to come any closer to the tree. "Doesn't it give you the heebie-jeebies?" he asked.

"What?" Lavender asked.

"Standing that close to a tree when you know a bear could be up any one of them?"

"Ugh, I didn't think of that," Lavender said, hopping away from the trunk.

Marisol and Rachelle followed her. Rachelle was in fits of laughter, saying, "Ew! Gross. I just had a thought. What if a bear was up there and went to the bathroom? Can you imagine getting hit with *that*?"

"It would be like a bomb went off," John said.

"Sick!" said Marisol.

"Bear bomb!" said John. He tossed a handful of pine cones high in the air. They soared in a steady parabola and rained down between the girls. Lavender and Rachelle scattered to avoid the pine cones, but Marisol's attention was on the hillside a few feet away.

"Look!" Marisol pointed to a massive prickly pear growing out of the dirt.

"Oh, that looks perfect," Lavender said. "But how do we eat one of these without stabbing ourselves?"

Marisol bit her bottom lip. "I've been thinking about that, but to be honest, I've never had one from the wild. We always just buy nopales from the grocery store."

"I have seen those at Fry's before," said Rachelle as she joined them to study the cactus. "But Marisol is right. They didn't have any thorns."

"I think the ones in the grocery store are a different variety," Marisol said.

"If we're careful, I guess we can scrape the thorns off with my knife," John said. "It'll be like peeling potatoes. Only with a bunch of spikes."

"What?" Rachelle asked him, voice full of shock. "You have a knife? On a school trip?"

"How come you didn't show us that when we did the inventory?" Marisol asked indignantly.

"For the same reason I didn't mention that I also have a lighter," John said. "I didn't want to hear you freak out about it."

"It's worth freaking out over. It's not safe," Rachelle snapped. "You're gonna get expelled."

Lavender snorted. "Who's going to expel him? The bear?"

John shrugged. "I'll worry about it if we get back. I mean when we get back," he corrected himself.

Marisol held out a hand. "I'll skin the prickly pear if you'll start a fire. That way we can grill them."

"Do we really have time for that?" Rachelle asked with an impatient glance toward the mountain.

Marisol bit her lip, looking uncertain.

"It's still early in the day," Lavender said. "We've been up since sunrise. It was probably like five a.m." At the same time her empty stomach let out a huge, rumbling growl.

"Sounds like we'd better make time," John said. "I can make a fire fast."

"It'll taste better," Marisol said. "Plus it would be nice to warm up."

"You know what else helps you stay warm? Walking."

"Cooking it might help kill germs," Marisol added with a shrewd look. "We don't have a way to wash them."

Rachelle bit her lip. "Fine."

Lavender blinked in surprise at how well Marisol

knew Rachelle. Marisol had said the exact right things to convince Rachelle.

"But we have to work fast," Rachelle said. "John and Lavender can get firewood. I'll help Marisol with peeling the cactus."

"You will?" Marisol sounded surprised.

"Yeah." Rachelle shrugged. "If we could survive tweezing our eyebrows for the first time, we can handle cactus needles."

What? Since when was Marisol getting her eyebrows done?

Even worse, for the first time, Lavender thought that maybe there was something real about Marisol's friendship with Rachelle. All along Lavender had assumed it was just shallow, some kind of warped alliance to punish her . . . for—for something. Lavender had always known that Rachelle had it out for her, and somehow Rachelle had sucked Marisol into her orbit of sixth-grade drama. Lavender had thought she just needed to separate them and things would snap back to normal.

Now Lavender wondered if showing Rachelle's true colors wouldn't work. In fact, it felt like Marisol already saw the real Rachelle, and Lavender was the one who'd misunderstood all along. Watching them help each other as they started using sticks to knock pieces of the cactus to the ground before skinning them left Lavender reeling. It transformed the gnawing hunger in Lavender's gut into something sharper and more painful: Marisol and Rachelle were acting like friends. Real friends.

19

John chose a little clearing away from any of the shrubs and with no tree branches directly overhead where they could have a fire. As a safety precaution, he kicked the fallen leaves and pine needles out of the way.

Lavender followed after him, feeling strangely subdued. There were times when she felt like Marisol was just growing up faster than her. And as they got older, their interests were getting more and more different . . . and there was nothing Lavender could do about it.

"Are you going to help, or are you just going to stand there?"

"Sorry," Lavender said as she realized that she

had been just staring while John did all the work. This was not the time to obsess over friend problems. She had even more important issues to work through . . . like how to not die. "Here's what we're going to do," she told John. "Let's split up to look for wood. We need any bigger branches or pieces of wood that are on the ground, but don't forget to check trees. We might be able to break a low branch off one of these pine trees."

Lavender headed in one direction, expecting John to go in the opposite direction. She knew her plan was perfectly logical, so she jerked back in surprise when he was suddenly striding alongside her.

"We're splitting up, remember?" she said.

"You've never played basketball, have you?"

What?

"Can we talk basketball later?" she asked.

"Just answer my question."

She glanced up toward the sky in exasperation and huffed. But John's mouth was a straight line and his eyebrows were drawn low and narrowed. He looked stubborn, and Lavender decided it would be faster to answer him than to argue with him.

"We're in the same class. You know I've played basketball in PE."

"No," he said. "I mean, like, on an actual team."

"Oh," said Lavender. "No."

If anything, his eyebrows drew even closer together. "What about soccer or softball or volleyball?"

Lavender shook her head. She didn't know where he was going with this, but she was impatient with the waste of time.

"Have you ever played on any team sport?"

"You've seen me in PE, right? I'm not very athletic." The words were short and sharp, and Lavender felt her mouth pinch together. She *hated* to admit she wasn't the best at anything. She wished she could catch a ball as effortlessly as she could multiply by fourteen. Lavender was the only sixth grader who had her times table memorized through the seventeens. She was working on the eighteens when even Mrs. Henderson used a calculator after the twelves.

John's stubborn look vanished, replaced by faint surprise. "It's not about being athletic."

"Easy for you to say."

A smile flashed across his face before he looked serious again. "It's about learning to be on a *team*. You know, letting people take turns doing what they're best at. If you always miss three-point shots and someone who is good at them is standing next to you, you pass the ball. If you're guarding number seven, you don't try to guard number fourteen. That's someone else's job. You have to let them do it."

Lavender's stomach rumbled. The empty ache reminded her that she'd only eaten trail mix and protein bars in the last twenty-four hours.

"Can we talk about this later?" Lavender asked. "If you'd just done what I said, we'd both have some firewood by now."

"No, what we'd have is some smoky wood that wouldn't burn and no kindling. We don't want green wood—nothing from a tree. We want really dry branches, so we should only get things from the ground, and we need dry pine needles and twigs, too. That's how we get the fire started."

"Oh." Lavender was both embarrassed and annoyed.

"And if you ask my opinion, we should stick together. Last time we split up, you found a bear. It might have mauled you if your backup wasn't there to save your butt."

She couldn't really argue with that. "I guess if you put it like that, maybe we should do it your way."

They walked in a big circle, sweeping the space around the makeshift firepit for twigs and dried pine needles and any fallen sticks or branches. Before long, they had a good size pile. Lavender brushed her hands together and looked at their handiwork with a smile.

"Not too bad," she said to John.

"It's a start."

"A start?"

"Yeah, it won't last that long."

"Aren't we kind of in a hurry?" Lavender reminded him.

He nodded. "From the sound of it, we have time to get more firewood."

Lavender shot a look toward Marisol and Rachelle and the pitifully small amount of cactus they'd skinned so far. It seemed like the prickly pear was fighting back, and it might even be winning.

Lavender sighed and turned to John. "We might as well," she said. If nothing else, at least moving around kept her from shivering. They walked in a wider circle. This time, they had even better luck. They found one huge branch. Since John didn't have an ax in his backpack, they took turns jumping on the dry wood and trying to snap it in pieces by holding one end while stomping on the other. Little shards of dried wood and sawdust flew in the air as they broke the bigger branch into more manageable pieces. Lavender only got one splinter. Unfortunately, it was the size of a railroad spike.

She studied the sliver of wood embedded in her palm. It throbbed painfully. She knew that was nothing compared to the sharp, stinging pain she would feel when she pulled it out.

"You don't have tweezers in your backpack, do you?"

"No, I didn't think of tweezers."

Lavender waved her hand and talked fast, trying to distract herself from the pain. "Go figure that you didn't bring tweezers. You have everything else. But I don't get it. Why did you bring all of it? Even the stuff that could get you in trouble with the teachers?"

"I guess I thought I might need it?"

"For what?" She waved her hand around more desperately. Not that it was really helping with the pain and suffering. At least this new, sharp pain meant she wasn't thinking about her dry throat or empty stomach anymore.

"If you let me see your hand, I'll tell you."

Lavender held out her hand and looked away, too squeamish to examine the massive chunk of wood protruding from her palm any closer.

John let out a low whistle. "Yikes, that is a bad one."

"I know that."

"The good thing is, it's big enough that I can just pull it out for you even without tweezers."

"No, don't." Lavender tried to yank her palm away, but John held tight, refusing to let her break free. "It's going to hurt," she said.

"It'll hurt worse if we leave it in there and it gets caught on something and rips."

"Okay." Lavender bit her lip, and after another quick glance at the splinter, she focused on a distant tree. "Just distract me. Tell me . . ." She tried to flash back to a time before the flood. "Tell me who you think stole the telescope money."

She felt John's hand tighten around hers. "I don't want to talk about that," he said.

"Fine, then something else. Like why you packed an entire Walmart store in your backpack."

"I will, but it's a secret." He spoke slowly as he shifted his hand into another position. Lavender fought to hold still. Her arm tensed as she imagined the tearing pain she was about to feel.

"Promise you won't tell," John said.

"I promise," Lavender said automatically. Any second now, he would grip the splinter and twist it out of her hand. Fire would shoot through her hand, her arm. *Don't think about how it's going to hurt*, she ordered herself. But it didn't work. The only thing she could think of was the pain.

John's fingers brushed over the palm of her hand.

He was about to pull it loose.

"Ready?" he said.

Lavender squeezed her eyes shut.

"I'm running away," he said.

When he pinched the piece of wood and ripped the splinter free from her flesh, she almost didn't feel it.

20

A pool of red blood blossomed on Lavender's hand in the hole left where the splinter used to be. Lavender pressed it against the front of her shirt, using her clothes to stem the blood flow. Already the pain was fading. It hurt but less intensely than seconds before. Dazedly, she stood there with the injured hand cradled to her chest. Had she heard John correctly?

"Did you say you're running away?"

He nodded slowly.

"From us?" Was he planning to desert her and Rachelle and Marisol? What about all that stuff he'd just said about teamwork?

This time, he shook his head.

"You mean . . . you were running away from . . ."

Her brain tried to put together the pieces. They were supposed to be on a field trip. Most people ran away from home, but was he saying he planned to run away from school? From the class? "Were you going to run away from science camp?"

His eyes darted to the side for a moment, as if he was trying to decide how to answer.

Lavender's hand throbbed. Her feet and throat and stomach ached. She didn't have the energy for games. "Just tell me the truth."

John shrugged, took a deep breath, and seemed to reach a decision. He spoke quickly and in a low voice. "I just thought that if I was going to run away from home, science camp would be the best place to do it."

That made absolutely no sense to Lavender. They were in the wilderness. No food. No shelter. No phone service. Even her radio had failed them in this isolated, endless stretch of land that couldn't quite decide if it was a desert or a forest.

"What were you thinking?" she said. "This is a terrible place to be stranded and on your own. Next time you run away, at least choose a place with *water.*"

"I wasn't planning to get lost in the middle of nowhere," he said. "I'm not that stupid. I was going to sneak away when we stopped in Willcox." Seeing the puzzled look on Lavender's face, he clarified, "The rest stop. Remember?"

"Yeah, but that's way outside of town. It's almost as bad as being out here."

"Not really," John said. "I'd just have to walk a few hours to get to a bus stop from there. I looked it up online."

"If that was your plan, why didn't you do it?"

"I might have, but then I wound up with a seat buddy." He gave her a pointed look. "I wanted to sit alone on the bus so I'd have a chance of disappearing without being noticed."

"What?"

"I know I wasn't very nice, but you kind of messed up my plan." He looked around with a faint smile. "I mean, that was the *first* time on this trip that you messed up my plan."

That made a weird kind of sense, and Lavender felt a little better. At least he hadn't turned into an angry hermit crab because he hated her; he just wanted the opportunity to sneak off without getting caught. It still didn't explain why someone so smart and talented and popular would want to run away.

"I guess I don't get it," Lavender said, pressing her

hand more firmly to the front of her shirt. "Why would you even want to run away? Did you have a fight with Kyle and Jeffrey?" She remembered how he'd been keeping his distance from them the previous day.

"What?" John said. "No."

"Oh, then why?" Sudden inspiration struck her. "Does it have to do with your parents fighting?"

John looked at ground and made a few scuff marks in the dirt and pine needles. "It doesn't really matter."

"It does to me."

"Why?"

"I don't know. It just does."

He didn't answer.

She tried again. "Because I've known you forever. You're in my class. I care about what happens to you. You're my friend."

He looked skeptical. "I wouldn't really say we're friends. It's not like we've ever hung out outside of school."

"What do you call this?" Lavender laughed and threw out her uninjured hand, gesturing at the pine trees around them. "We're not in school now. We escaped from a flood together. You saved my life when I was about to get attacked by a bear. You pulled a splinter out of my hand. If that doesn't make us friends, I don't know what will."

A breeze whispered through the pines above them. Otherwise, all was silent. The quiet stretched so long that Lavender was about to give up on an answer. And when John did finally speak, he looked as surprised as Lavender felt.

His words come out in a rush like water breaking through a dam. "I was going to visit my brother. He's in college, and he's doing this semester at a school in Monterrey, Mexico. I can take a bus there from Willcox. I just had to get to the bus station, and then I could go see him. I needed to get away from home. Ever since he left, it's been really, really bad. My parents told me they're getting a divorce, but nothing's changed. They still live in the same house; they scream and yell and fight all the time. I think they hate each other. Sometimes I think they even hate me, but Jackson doesn't. And I miss him so, so much."

He stopped then, and a little siren went off in Lavender's head: a warning sound, similar to the red alert from *Star Trek*. He looked like he was going to cry, and she did not know what to say or do.

This wasn't something she could fix. This wasn't something she could make better.

After a moment, she said the only thing she could think of. "I'm sorry."

"For what? It's not your fault."

"I know. I'm just sorry that that's happening to you. It sucks."

He kicked the ground once, hard. A low cloud of dust filled the air, then settled. "It does."

Lavender pulled her hand from her chest and awkwardly examined the cut.

"You look like you were shot in the chest."

"What?" Lavender looked down. The front of her T-shirt was smeared with blood. "Oh no," she said. "Do you think I'll attract bears and mountain lions? Are they like sharks? Do you think they can smell blood?"

"I don't think so," John said, "but if you're worried, you can wear my sweatshirt."

That made her feel better.

"Lavender! John!" Rachelle's voice echoed through the high desert.

"Where are you?" Marisol's shout joined Rachelle's.

"Coming," Lavender answered as loud as she could.

"We should get as much of this as we can." John

waved a hand at the scattered pieces of firewood that they'd broken off the tree branch.

Lavender nodded.

He carried most of the wood—she couldn't hold as much while trying to protect her cut hand from more splinters, dirt, and debris. As they made their way back to the ring for their campfire Lavender asked, "How were you going to pay for the bus ticket?"

"Oh." He shifted his armful of branches and twigs. "I had some money."

"How much is a ticket to Mexico from here?"

"Uh—" He looked away, then said very quickly, "It's pretty expensive."

"How expensive?"

"Like more than a hundred dollars."

Lavender was impressed. She wondered how he'd gotten that much money. Maybe his parents gave him a really good allowance, or he'd been saving up all of his birthday money. Before she could ask, they were interrupted by both Rachelle and Marisol, who shrieked in horror and sprinted over to help her when they saw the blood smeared all over Lavender's shirt.

21

As they sat at the foot of the mountain, the last of the morning chill disappeared. Lavender warmed her hands by the fire as they grilled the cactus on sticks. Marisol's idea had been a stroke of genius.

The nopales were slimy, and it was hard to keep them on the sticks. But everyone was so hungry that they agreed it was worth any amount of time and trouble once they skewered the cactus and cooked it. When a piece fell, they picked it right back up and ate it even with the dirt still on it. Except for Rachelle. When she dropped a cactus sliver on the ground, she gave it away and started over again.

The texture was mushy and a little sour. The

flavor reminded Lavender of a cross between aspar-
agus, lemon, and a pickle. Marisol said she'd had
better—the wild ones cooked over a campfire were
different than what she'd eaten from the store.

But no one complained. The cactus was moist. It
felt like a smooth balm on Lavender's dry lips. She
savored each bite, trying to suck the water from it
and letting the texture fill her mouth with saliva.
Nothing would have tasted as good as a glass of cool,
clean water. But this was the next best thing. Her
bottle was almost down to the last quarter, and
with a quick glance around the circle, Lavender saw
that no one else was doing much better. Rachelle's
was the lowest of all. She had maybe two or three
sips left.

"When we get back," Marisol said, "I'll ask my
grandma to make her sopa de nopales for you so you
can see what it's supposed to taste like."

"Is she a good cook?" Rachelle asked.

"The best," Marisol answered, and Lavender nodded. She'd had more than one of Marisol's grandma's
home-cooked meals.

"I can't wait to try it," said Rachelle. Lavender
looked at her in surprise. That was the last thing
she expected Rachelle to say after the way she used

to make fun of Marisol for basically everything. Maybe Rachelle had changed . . . People could change, couldn't they? "But if I could eat anything right now . . ." Rachelle continued. "I would ask my mom to take me to Dutch Bros for a large mango smoothie with passion fruit drizzle and extra whipped cream."

"I bet she'd do it," Marisol said.

"What?"

"Take you anywhere you want to go," Marisol said. "They're probably so worried about us."

Lavender nodded. For a second, Lavender let herself think of her parents. She would bet any amount of money that they were already helping to search for her or, at least, in their car on the way to Chiricahua.

John was silent. He stared directly into the fire, avoiding eye contact with all of them and saying nothing about his parents. With a little flash of insight, Lavender realized that this must be a really awkward conversation for him. After what he had told her, she knew his home life wasn't very good just now. So she tried to change the subject, saying, "Hey, John, you didn't say what you would eat. You know, if you could have anything right now?"

He looked up from the fire, his expression dazed, but after a few seconds, he smiled at Lavender and said, "Oh, um, I'd probably ask my older brother to take me to Outback. I want a steak and a Bloomin' Onion and a Coke. Or water, actually. Lots and lots of water."

"I love Outback," said Lavender. "But right now, I'd ask my dad to make his three-cheese risotto. I could eat an entire pan of it."

"It sounds really *gouda*," John said.

Lavender laughed.

"I don't get it," Rachelle said.

"Gouda is a kind of cheese," Marisol explained.

"Seriously? That is such a dad joke," Rachelle said.

"Yeah," John agreed. "It's *cheesy* enough for a dad joke."

By the time they had cooked every last bit of the cactus that Marisol and Rachelle had managed to skin and John put out the fire, Lavender was feeling energized and optimistic. She was ready to climb the mountain: blisters, sore muscles, cuts and scrapes and everything else. She just knew that the four of them could get to the top and get help. Whether they found a trail or hikers or got a cell signal, it was time to get out of this wilderness.

Now if only . . .

Rachelle would keep her mouth shut about sardines . . .

And they didn't collapse of dehydration . . .

And they didn't run into any other wild animals or natural disasters . . .

Then they might all have a chance at living long enough to make it to seventh grade.

But as they climbed up the mountain and the harsh reality of midday set in, Lavender did not see how they would ever make it. She wished she'd saved some of the nopales to eat as they climbed. It hadn't even occurred to her while they sat around the fire, feeling full and triumphant from scaring away a bear. She shouldn't have eaten so much or so quickly. The meal churned in her stomach, making her nauseous and desperately thirsty. Maybe if she'd saved it to eat slowly, Lavender wouldn't be so miserable now.

She tried to ration sips of her water, and she managed not to say "I told you so" when Rachelle paused next to a tree with bark so rough and patchy it looked like alligator skin and held up her Hydro Flask.

Rachelle unscrewed it and tipped it.

At first, Lavender's heart lurched into her throat. She thought Rachelle's mind had snapped under the pressure and she was dumping out her water supply on purpose. But nothing came out. Not a single drop.

Lavender knew that yesterday she would have rubbed it in. "What did you expect when you wasted it on cleaning your feet?" But somehow, today, Rachelle seemed like less of an archnemesis and more like an uneasy ally. She still resented Rachelle, but she was also starting to see a side of her that she could almost respect.

"Here." Lavender held out her own water bottle.

With a small smile, Rachelle took it and drank a sip.

"Don't take too much," Lavender said. It was down to the last eighth; two or three gulps, and it would be gone. Rachelle took only one small swallow and handed it back. They all took turns sharing with her as they continued the ascent, searching desperately around every curve in the terrain for a trail or a backpacker or any hint of rescue.

The day dragged on with no sign of help, and Lavender started to feel as if she'd been on that mountain her entire life. With each plodding step, her head pounded. Her hands felt heavy, swollen, and irritated. She did not know if it was from the splinter or from dehydration or something else altogether. Rachelle was repeatedly claiming that dehydration could cause swollen fingers, but what did she know? And how, Lavender wondered, was she still talking so much?

As the climb grew steeper and more treacherous, the others had fallen silent. Lavender assumed that, like her, they were suffering from a terribly dry throat and also breathlessness. Lavender continuously looked from side to side, trying to measure the ascent of the mountain against the horizon so she could mentally calculate the angle they were climbing. To her aching muscles, it felt like a ninety-degree climb, but she knew that was not possible: They were not on a sheer cliff face. Realistically, she calculated it was probably closer to a twenty-five-degree angle—steeper in some places and less steep in others, but that was her guess.

She was probably wildly wrong. Not because she was bad at mental math, but because she was exhausted. The bone-deep fatigue pulled at her arms and legs, pounded on her brain, and made clear thought impossible until all she could think of was putting one foot in front of the other. There was no room for thought beyond taking the next step.

Pausing for a rest, halfway up the mountain, Lavender crouched in the shade of a large boulder. She unscrewed her water bottle and lifted it to her lips, but it was empty.

22

When Lavender was in fifth grade, her class had taken a trip to the Arizona Science Center, and during the educational program, one of the museum employees dipped a tennis ball in liquid nitrogen and then hit it with a hammer. The ball shattered into tiny frozen fragments.

As Lavender stared into her empty water bottle, she felt like someone had frozen her with liquid nitrogen and then smashed her with a hammer into tiny shards that could never be put back together again.

"Does anyone have any water left?" she called in a hoarse voice to the others, who were sitting nearby.

Marisol and Rachelle shook their heads. John

held up his water bottle and swished it around. "I've got enough for maybe one sip each."

Lavender blinked. John's bottle reflected in the sunlight and hurt her eyes.

"No, it's your water," Marisol told John. "You should drink it."

But John shook his head. "It's okay. I'll share. Here, Lavender."

Head pounding, Lavender forced herself to walk the few steps to John.

"We're already dehydrated," Rachelle was saying. "We definitely haven't been drinking the amount that a person needs, especially when you're doing as much physical activity as we are. At this point, a couple of drops aren't going to make a difference."

"Then I'll drink your share," Lavender said. She was so parched that every drop felt like it was the difference between life and death. But when she took John's bottle, Lavender only let herself take one small sip. In silence, she passed it to Marisol, who took a sip, then to John, who took a sip before passing it to Rachelle.

In spite of her words, Rachelle pressed the bottle to her lips, but she did not finish the water like Lavender had expected. Rachelle left enough for

John to drink the final drops. But he didn't. In grim silence, John screwed the cap back on, and they stood and continued their climb.

Lavender felt a heavy weight descend over the group. Her confidence had completely dried up. They were in serious trouble. They were getting dangerously close to the twenty-four-hour mark that Marisol had told her about.

Only Rachelle was in denial. She chattered without pausing as they maneuvered between rocks and scrabbled uphill. Lavender grew almost dizzy listening to Rachelle bounce from one topic to the next. She blathered about her blisters, her soccer team, her favorite YouTube channel, her lost phone, which she thought had a warranty, and even the class's missing telescope money. Rachelle tried to get everyone to say what they thought had happened to it, but Lavender didn't make a guess. She was breathing too hard to bother with words.

Before long, Lavender stopped paying any attention. Rachelle's one-sided conversation blurred into a haze of background noise, which lasted until Marisol's voice broke through. She said exactly what Lavender had been thinking: "How do you even have enough energy to keep talking?"

The entire group came to a halt.

"I guess I'm in really good shape."

"So's John," Lavender croaked, thinking of all the sports he played, "but he's not talking a mile a minute."

"My throat is too dry to talk," John said.

In answer, Rachelle poked a lumpy yellowish-brown object out between her front teeth.

"What is that?" he asked.

"It's a pebble."

"But why is it in your mouth?" Marisol said slowly, as if she was talking to someone on the brink of a mental breakdown.

"Relax," Rachelle said. "It's just a trick my grandpa told me about. If you're thirsty and there's no water, you can suck on a rock."

"Oh, I think I've heard of that before," said John. "Isn't it an old trick soldiers used?"

"Yeah, you get a lot more saliva in your mouth," Rachelle said. "Then you don't feel as thirsty."

"That's not going to stop us from being dehydrated," said Lavender.

"No, it won't," Rachelle agreed. "But it's better than nothing."

"Heck, I'll try anything," said John.

He and Marisol both bent to find rocks. Lavender wasn't so sure.

"Don't you think it's a bad idea?" she said. "What if you inhale it and choke?"

"I know the Heimlich maneuver," Rachelle said.

"Or you bite down and crack a tooth?"

Rachelle shrugged. "I'm not saying it's a good option. We ran out of those when the flood tried to wipe us all off the face of the Earth."

Lavender's head throbbed. Her face and neck hurt from yesterday's sunburn. In fact, it was probably time to reapply her sunscreen, but her arms wouldn't work. She couldn't even search for a pebble like the others, because if she squatted down, she wasn't sure if she would get up again. Resting her forehead against a nearby pine tree, she took deep, even breaths, trying to stave off the crushing fatigue and looming panic.

"Here." Marisol stuck a pebble in her hand. "You should try it. It really is better than nothing." Lavender tightened her fist around the rock.

"Let's keep going," John said. His voice was already less raspy than it had been only a few minutes before. "If we want to reach the top before night, we shouldn't stop too long."

As they began climbing, Lavender slipped the pebble between her dry lips. Moisture filled her mouth. It helped. Lavender tried to take even breaths without any sudden gasping or inhaling. She didn't want to choke to death on a rock. She didn't want to die, even though it was sinking in that she was closer to death than she'd ever been in her life.

With every grueling step, Lavender continued searching for a trail. She scoured the mountainside for any sign of human life: a trail, a tent, a bench—even litter would have been a welcome sight in that moment, some sort of tangible proof that they were not the only four humans left on the planet.

There was none.

No wrappers.

No plastic bottles.

No wadded-up papers.

Normally, Lavender would have loved to see such a beautiful, pristine landscape. It was a miracle to find a corner of Earth so untouched.

But the very remoteness of the area filled her with a nameless dread. If they didn't reach the mountaintop and find a trail, or see a ranger station, or get a radio or cell signal, then all hope was lost.

She poked the rock around with her tongue. The pebble was a lumpy oval with some rough patches and some smooth. As much as she hated to give Rachelle credit for anything, it was helping.

But Lavender did not thank Rachelle. She didn't say anything. As the afternoon wore on, even Rachelle gave up on speech. They were exhausted, weary, and scared.

Then there came a part of the hike so steep that Lavender wanted to cry. Here, a few of the angles had to be a for real ninety degrees, and they were no longer hiking but scaling rocks. Lavender's hand—raw from the splinter—hurt with a sharp, stabbing pain that only increased when she had to pull and tug against boulders.

She was ready to quit, when John called out: "The peak! I can see it. We're almost there."

He was just a few feet ahead of her, standing on the edge of boulders so steep that it made her stomach drop.

"Be careful!" she called to him. "Don't stand so close to the edge."

"Come on," he called down to her. "You've got this."

But Lavender was utterly exhausted. With barely

any food or water all day, she was nearly at the end of her stamina. Next to her, Marisol looked equally frail. Rachelle was just ahead of them, perched on a rock a few feet above their own. She twisted to look at them. "You guys, he's right. I see it. We're so close to the peak."

"Go on ahead without us," said Marisol. She flopped her hand in an exhausted wave, shooing Rachelle away.

"No, not without you," Rachelle said. "Leave no man behind."

"What?" asked Lavender. She tried to clear her head with a little shake. It didn't help; it only made the pounding worse.

"Something else my grandpa used to say. I think from when he was in the army."

"Why are we talking about your grandpa?" Lavender asked.

"Because we're not leaving you behind."

"Why do you even care?"

"Because you look like you're about to pass out," Rachelle retorted. "I'm not leaving anyone when they look like that. So get your butts up here, both of you, or John and I will drag you the rest of the way up the mountain." When neither Lavender nor

Marisol moved, Rachelle turned around and called, "John! Come back."

Rachelle gestured to him. He'd been leaning in the shade of a large boulder, waiting for them to catch up. Now he climbed back down. Lavender didn't know how he did it. She couldn't imagine making that climb once, never mind twice.

Lavender rolled the pebble around in her mouth, trying to moisten her throat. She was parched. Her mouth was a desert. The Sahara was a tropical paradise compared to her.

With a thud, John landed on the ground in front of her.

He reached in his backpack and grimly handed Lavender his water bottle. The last sip still swished around in it. She shook her head. She couldn't drink the last of the water.

But he just held out his arm until she took it.

Spitting out the pebble, she unscrewed the cap and let the last bit of water drain into her mouth. It was the single most generous thing anyone had ever done for her, and it gave Lavender the strength to force herself to her feet even as Rachelle limped over to Marisol and heaved her up.

Once she started moving, a little of Lavender's

energy came back to her, and she found the strength to make it over the last few boulders. Maybe it was because Rachelle and John helped, calling encouragement and holding out a hand anytime a little extra effort was needed. They took a few rests, but Lavender did not make the mistake of sitting, leaning, or slumping over again. She knew they might really end up having to drag her if she did that.

At the last stop, when all four of them had a perfect view of the mountain peak, she turned to Rachelle and said, "Thanks for helping me. I know you don't like me."

"You don't like me," Rachelle said.

The first thought to pop into Lavender's mind was *I don't.*

They had never been friends. Rachelle had rubbed Lavender the wrong way since the first time she'd shown up at Wellson Elementary. When she'd introduced herself to the class on her first day as a new student, she'd stood in front of everyone and said, "My name is Rachelle Winchester, and my parents enrolled me at this school because they're old friends with the principal." She could be a smug little know-it-all.

Now Lavender found herself wondering whether Rachelle must have felt the same way about her.

Before she could muster enough energy to ask, Rachelle answered the unspoken look stamped across Lavender's face.

"You don't have to like someone to do what's right," Rachelle said. "Doctors don't have to like their patients. Teachers don't have to like their students. Waiters don't have to like their customers."

"But it helps," said Marisol, "when people like each other and are nice."

"Yeah," John agreed in a faraway voice, "it does." And Lavender wondered if he was thinking about his parents.

Studying the three faces around her—streaked with dirt and scraped from running through the wilderness and chapped from the dry climate— Lavender felt a wave of affection for these three. Straightening her shoulders, she heard herself make a sudden vow: "Get me out of the wilderness alive, and I'll never lie again and I'll like all of you until the day I die. Seriously, you'll be my best friends no matter what. I'll have your backs for-ev-er." She didn't care if they believed her; in that moment, she knew she meant every syllable of it.

"Dramatic much?" Marisol asked with a weary smile, but Lavender heard a familiar teasing tone—the one Marisol used with her best friends. And Lavender found herself smiling, too. Marisol staggered a few steps forward. "Come on, we can see the peak. We're almost there. I just know we're going to see our campsite or find a trail or a backpacker or something. I can feel it."

A light, bubbly feeling rose up in Lavender's chest. It took her a few seconds to recognize the emotion. It was hope.

23

They crested the last rise, only to find a barren mountain peak.

"Where's the camp?" Rachelle asked, looking in every direction. "We should be able to see it from here. I *know* this is the mountain we could see from our campsite."

Lavender turned in a slow circle, checking in every direction. Spread out below them was an incredible view. If she'd had food and water and a map, maybe she would have appreciated it. Mile after mile of spectacular scenery . . . as far as her eyes could see there were mountains, trees, rock spires, and—she took it in with a feeling of despair—a vast untouched wilderness.

"Stay calm. We all just need to stay calm," John ordered, and Lavender wondered if he was talking to Rachelle or to himself. "We knew we might not find someone here, but I bet the reception will be better. I'm going to try my phone. I'm sure we can get a signal from up here."

"And I've got my radio!" Lavender said.

Lavender dug it out of her backpack and turned it on with shaking hands. Nothing.

She held her breath as John powered up his cell phone. It felt like an eternity as the screen lit up and slowly turned on. The display shone: 3:43 p.m. Their twenty-four hours were up.

If Marisol's mom's TV shows were right, they weren't ever going to be found.

John began dialing 911 over and over again.

There was no answer. There was no signal. Still.

Lavender tried her radio. Same result as before. The last remaining bubble of hope in Lavender's chest burst and oozed into something dark and heavy and terrifying, weighing down every limb. She collapsed onto her knees and rested her forehead on the hot ground. So that was it.

"There has to be a trail. Some sort of trail. We just didn't cross it," John said, dashing a little way down

the peak. "Maybe on the other side of the mountain."
Lavender stayed glued to her spot in the dirt.

She heard Marisol say, "Didn't Mr. Gonzales say that some areas mark trails with little piles of rocks or spray paint on rocks and trees? Maybe we didn't see the trail because we're expecting to see a path, and we just weren't looking for the right thing."

Meanwhile, John was growing frantic. "No! No! No!" he said as he sped by her again and rushed in another direction, still vainly searching for a trail, a path, a campsite, a backpacker.

It was useless. They were doomed.

Lavender couldn't make herself get up to help. There was no point looking for something that wasn't there. Her head pounded. Lavender flopped onto her back. It no longer mattered if she could get up. She would never move again. This was it.

Using her backpack as a pillow, Lavender studied the clouds overhead. The sky was still thick with them. They were moving quickly, racing across the sky, furling and unfurling in billows like puffs of smoke. She wished she could reach out and scoop the particles into her hand. Instead they taunted her. Thousands of feet above her, out of reach, she could see them—huge bursts of ice particles. She was going to die of thirst, while looking at exquisite works of art made of water.

Life was cruel.

And short.

Well, hers would be short. Sixth graders were supposed to worry about being bored in school and having too much homework and if their crush liked them back and who to invite to their birthday party. Sixth graders were not supposed to be worried about whether or not they would have enough food or clean water or how they were going to die.

Lost in her own thoughts, Lavender ignored the others. She had no idea how much time had passed when a shadow fell across her face. Marisol was standing over her.

"Any luck?" Lavender asked, already sure of a negative answer. "Did you find anything?"

"No," said Marisol. "But thanks for all your help." She plopped into the dirt beside Lavender.

"I'm sorry. I'm just too tired and thirsty to move."

"How do you think the rest of us feel?" But Marisol leaned back, planting her head on the backpack next to Lavender's. "Scoot over. Give me some room."

"Where are Rachelle and John?" Lavender asked.

"John decided to try digging for water. He

remembers seeing a survival show where people in the desert dug a hole at the base of a tree or something and found a puddle of water."

"Wouldn't it be all muddy and gross?' asked Lavender.

"Who cares? At this point, I'd drink mud water."

"Me too." Lavender paused.

"I'd drink anything," Marisol said.

"Even urine?"

"Honestly, I thought about that. I've heard sailors used to do that if they ran out of water."

"I don't want to."

"Me either."

"What if it means the difference between life and death?" asked Lavender.

"Then I guess we're going to die," said Marisol with a weak attempt at a chuckle.

Lavender tried to laugh, too, but she couldn't. She was afraid if she showed any hint of emotion, she was going to be swallowed up by all of them—but mostly despair.

"Where's Rachelle? Is she helping John?" Lavender asked.

She felt, rather than saw, Marisol shake her head.

"What's she doing?"

Marisol sighed. "She's losing her mind. I think she might actually be having a breakdown. When we couldn't find any trails or anything, she just went berserk. I tried to help her, but she told me to leave her alone. I think she was crying, but there were, like, no tears. It was freaky."

Crying without tears.

That sounded bad. They must be really dehydrated if that was the case. Lavender had two choices: She could just lie there until something killed her or—

"I should probably get up and do something," Lavender said. "Like help John dig."

"Yeah," said Marisol. "Me too."

Neither of them moved. They lay there in silence. Lavender didn't know what Marisol was doing, but Lavender was watching the clouds again. They had morphed into new shapes, startling in beauty and a haunting reminder of everything she was about to lose. She closed her eyes for a minute, just remembering, listening to the sound of Marisol's breathing and wondering how long her parents would keep looking for her after she gave up. She missed them, but she was fiercely, selfishly glad that she was not alone on this mountaintop. "I'm glad you're here with me," Lavender said.

Marisol didn't say anything, and Lavender allowed her own eyes to drift closed. A few seconds passed, and Lavender heard her friend shift. Marisol's hand closed around one of Lavender's own.

24

Exhaustion pushed on her, and Lavender drifted into an uneasy nap with Marisol beside her. Eventually, John joined them. The sound of his heavy, defiant footsteps pulled Lavender from her light sleep. She cracked open an eye and studied him.

John was scowling. His hands were dirty and covered in mud. He was dragging his backpack on the ground by one of its straps. When Marisol sat up and asked in a tired voice if he'd found anything, he threw his backpack with so much force that Lavender worried it would sail right off the mountain.

Then he tossed himself into the dirt next to them and said, "I give up. All those survival shows are just a bunch of rotten lies."

"If it was easy, more people would do it," said Marisol.

Lavender said nothing. She was starting to get cold again. It made sense that the temperature would be even lower on top of a mountain. They had all been so convinced that they'd be rescued once they reached the top that none of them even considered what it would be like to stay overnight at that elevation.

But after a long rest, Lavender's head hurt less. She was still exhausted, hungry, and, most of all, thirsty, but she felt good enough after her nap to push herself up. She stood too quickly and for a moment, the entire world spun, but after a few deep breaths, everything righted itself.

"What are you doing?" Marisol asked.

"Firewood," said Lavender. After her long rest, it turned out that she wasn't ready to just give up.

"Good idea." Marisol dragged herself to her feet. "I can feel the temperature dropping."

"Need help?" John asked. His voice was still hard and angry.

"No, we've got it," said Lavender. "We rested while you were working."

"Cool," said John with as much expression as

an amoeba. Lavender had a feeling that she could have told him that she was going to sprout wings and fly them all to safety and she would have gotten the same unconcerned answer.

Lavender and Marisol walked all around the mountaintop, collecting any sticks, twigs, dried leaves, and shrub they could find.

"Ouch!" said Marisol, suddenly dropping the stick she'd reached under a bush for.

"What? Are you okay?" Lavender asked.

"Yeah, it's just the prickles from skinning the cactus. There were all these super-fine, tiny thorns that got stuck in my hands. We could avoid the bigger ones, but the almost invisibles ones got everywhere, and they really hurt if I brush them the wrong way against something."

"Thirty-seven," said Lavender.

Marisol picked up the stick, more gingerly this time. "What?"

"That's your score. I've been keeping track of how many times you complain about the prickly pear thorns."

"Ha! Well, I was counting, too, while we climbed the mountain. I was just too nice to say it out loud." She gave Lavender a very serious look. "One thousand two hundred and eleven. That's how many times you've complained about the cut on your hand."

They were still making up fake numbers when they returned to the peak, where John was stretched out. He'd wiped some of the mud from his hands and flashlight. Lavender could clearly see what he'd done, because now the dirt was smeared across his shirt—not that his T-shirt had been clean before . . .

John was still lying on his back, face toward the clouds, turning the flashlight on and off. On and off. On and off. On and off.

Marisol, her arms full of firewood, stopped beside him. "Aren't you worried about wasting the battery?"

"Actually," Lavender cut in, "it's not the worst idea. If you wait until dark and then turn it on and off three times real fast, then three times only leave it on longer, and then three more fast times, that's the international distress signal in Morse code. If a plane or helicopter comes close enough, maybe they'll see it and know we need help."

John snorted. "And maybe the Phoenix Suns will win the NBA Finals."

"Since when did you learn Morse code?" Marisol asked Lavender, ignoring John.

"I don't actually know it other than SOS, because it's so famous." She turned back to John. "Here, give me the light. I'll show you."

"What's the point?" John said. "We're never getting off this mountain anyway."

Even though Lavender had been feeling the same way, hearing someone else say it out loud made her realize that she wasn't ready to give up.

"You can do whatever you want," Lavender said. "But I'm making a fire. If we're lucky, someone will see it and come investigate. If we're unlucky, at least we won't freeze as we die. Now give me your lighter."

"Get the lighter yourself," he said. "You know where my backpack is."

"I will," she said to John. Then she turned to Marisol. "Do you want to clear a space for the fire while I get the lighter?"

Marisol nodded and went to work while Lavender opened John's backpack, wishing it was a magical Mary Poppins bag. She imagined reaching inside to find a hot meal, a working radio, sleeping bags and coats for everyone, and gallons of water.

Instead, the first thing she saw was an empty

water bottle. Then his jacket. Then maps, three of them, including one of Mexico, and also a Greyhound bus schedule. She shook her head. Surely, he'd had his fill of being on his own and had changed his mind about running away by now. If they got back— no, *when* they got back—she would help him come up with a better solution to his family problems than running away. There was nothing else in the main compartment. The lighter must have been in the front pocket of the bag.

Lavender unzipped it and immediately spotted the lighter. She took it out, but next to the lighter, she saw something unexpected. Something that wasn't supposed to be there.

"Not the front pocket." John had suddenly sat up as if he'd realized something. He was yelling even though he was only a few feet away. "I'll get it. Don't look in the front pocket."

He was too late.

Lavender had already pulled out the crumpled envelope full of cash. She recognized the handwriting on that envelope. It was their teacher's, and it was clearly marked *$ for our telescope!*

25

It took a moment for Lavender to understand what she held in her hand. At first, it simply would not compute. She could read the words on the envelope. She could feel the wad of cash inside. Logically, Lavender knew there was only one reasonable explanation. But she could not make herself understand it. She didn't want to.

$ for our telescope!

This was the cash that had gone missing after the bake sale.

$ for our telescope!

John had the money.

$ for our telescope!

John was the thief. She didn't want to believe it.

Only a handful of seconds had ticked by since she'd discovered the money, but it felt like hours. She felt betrayed. Lavender had trusted John. It wasn't until that moment that she realized that, somewhere in the wilderness, she had really, truly started to think of him as a friend.

He'd left the safety of the class to help her get Rachelle and Marisol. He'd stayed calm when it felt like everything else was crashing down around them. He'd magically provided solutions: a flashlight, a sweatshirt, a pocketknife, a lighter. He'd gotten the splinter out of her hand. He'd shared the last of his water. And he'd confided in her, told her about the problems at home. Lavender had thought that he trusted her as much as she trusted him.

As all this raced through Lavender's mind, John finally put down his flashlight and sprinted over. When he saw what was in her hand, he came to a complete stop, his face ashen.

"I can ex—" he started to say.

But Lavender didn't want to hear any of it.

"No, don't. Just don't. I'm just going to—"

Lavender was going to shove the envelope back to the bottom of his bag and forget about it. Maybe forever. Maybe just until they got home. If they ever got home . . . She only knew one thing for certain: It wouldn't do anyone any good to talk about it now. They had other, bigger problems to solve. Like staying alive.

Before she could make it disappear, she heard footsteps behind her. If possible, John's eyes grew even wider. And then the envelope was snatched out of her hand.

Lavender whirled around. What she saw was even more terrifying than an angry bear. Rachelle stood there, leaves and sticks stuck in her hopelessly tangled curls. Fresh dirt was smudged along one cheek. Her eyes were red and puffy, but there were no tear tracks running down her face.

"What is this?" she asked.

Lavender did not answer. She was pretty confident that—having read the envelope—Rachelle knew exactly what it was.

"It's—it's—" John tried to answer.

"I know what it is!" Rachelle said, her voice shrill. "The real question is how did it get here?"

From the corner of her eye, Lavender could see Marisol inching closer.

"I . . ." John trailed off. He was having trouble forming words.

"What's going on?" Marisol asked, her voice quiet and even.

"We're gonna die! We're lost and stranded and we're going to die with these—with these jerks!" Rachelle stormed over to Marisol and waved the envelope in front of her face.

John stared at the ground, unable to make eye contact. His shoulders were slumped. Lavender thought that she had never seen someone look so defeated and beaten down.

"He took the money our class raised for the telescope! He's a thief."

"Rachelle," Marisol said. "Calm down."

Lavender held a hand up to her temple. Her headache was coming back.

"You want me to calm down? I said we're going to *die* if you haven't noticed."

"Well, this isn't helping," Lavender said. She tried to copy Marisol's rational tone, but the words came out sounding sarcastic.

"This is just great!" Rachelle threw her hands in the air. The envelope flew out of them, showering cash everywhere. The ones, fives, and tens rained down on the foursome, and a little breeze blew the money in different directions, scattering the paper across the stone. No one moved to pick it up. "I can't believe I'm going to die with the two of you." She pointed at John. "A thief!" She pointed at Lavender. "And a liar!"

"Don't call Lavender names," said Marisol. "It's not her fault John messed up."

Those were the words Lavender had been desperate to hear. Ever since the concert, she'd wondered if she'd lost her best friend forever. Now, at the absolute lowest and worst possible time, Marisol was finally defending her. When Lavender didn't deserve it at all. Her chest felt like it was cracking in two. She tried to swallow, but her throat was too dry. Lavender knew she'd made a mistake. A big one. Possibly beyond repair.

"I'm not talking about the money," said Rachelle.

"Let's just all get some wood and start the fire," Lavender said, desperate to change the subject. "It's getting cold."

"You don't even know," Rachelle said to Marisol. "You still think she's your friend."

"And water," said Lavender, holding out her hands toward Rachelle, begging her to drop the subject. "We should try to come up with a plan to find water."

Rachelle ignored Lavender's plea.

"It's Lavender's fault we're stuck out here. It's her fault we're lost."

"No, it's not," Marisol said. "She saved us, and you know it. Lavender *and* John, they saved us from the flood."

"We never would have been separated from the rest of the group if Lavender hadn't lied."

"About what?" Marisol wanted to know.

"Ask her."

Marisol turned to Lavender, and there was a question on Marisol's face. More than anything, Lavender wanted to deny what Rachelle said, but she couldn't. It would only make everything worse if she lied again, if she lied about this.

"What is she talking about?" asked Marisol.

"I didn't know there was going to be a flash flood." Lavender looked down, trying to find the right words to explain. "I never would have—"

"Tell her," Rachelle interrupted. "Tell her how you wanted to get back at me because you were jealous that Marisol had another friend. You're too selfish to let Marisol be friends with anyone else. So you tried to make us look like a couple of losers, hiding when no one was looking for us."

"You did what?" Marisol asked.

"It was so stupid. It was just supposed to be a prank," Lavender said.

"There wasn't really a game of sardines?"

Slowly, Lavender shook her head.

Marisol took a step back.

"It's not as bad as it sounds," said Lavender. Her head felt like a vise was tightening around it. She tried to ignore the pain.

Marisol said, "I thought it was all my fault that we were stranded out here. Rachelle and I were so far away from the rest of the group because of where I wanted to hide, but you—you—" She took another step away. Lavender reached out a hand to stop her. Marisol flinched. "Don't. I just need a few minutes."

"Wait," said Lavender. "Let me explain."

"Not now. I can't even look at you." And Marisol darted off toward the bushes where John had been digging for water. Lavender started to go after her. She would explain. Marisol would listen. She had to.

Rachelle stepped in front of Lavender. "Leave her alone."

"Get out of my way," said Lavender.

"Just leave us alone," Rachelle said.

"No, I really want to explain." Lavender didn't know how, but she had to make things right.

Rachelle shook her head, and then she said, "If you really want to help, why don't you build that fire and then . . . I don't know, pray that we get rescued, because otherwise we're all goners."

Lavender stayed rooted in place and watched Rachelle follow after Marisol. She wanted to cry, but that would take entirely too much energy and would probably only make her headache worse. Instead, she started slowly picking up the dollar bills that were scattered all over the mountaintop. She wondered how they would taste. A kid in her fourth-grade class used to eat paper sometimes, but Lavender didn't think it could have much nutritional value. It would probably just make her sick. Maybe she could use them for kindling if they were having trouble starting the fire.

When she'd gathered up the money, she looked at the bills again. She'd never held so much cash in her life. It wouldn't do her any good now. At home, Lavender could have bought enough food and water for three weeks. Out here, money was absolutely useless. In the wilderness, it didn't matter how much money you had—or didn't have—everyone was equal. They were all just fighting to stay alive.

Lavender shoved the cash in her back pocket.

The breeze picked up, and a shiver ran down Lavender's spine. With every second, the sun sank lower and the temperature dropped. It was only as she walked over to the fire ring, lighter in hand, that she realized she was truly alone. John was gone.

26

"John!" she called. Her voice echoed off the stone, but there was no reply.

Lavender cupped her hands to make her voice go farther.

"John!" she called again.

Still no answer.

She ran back and forth around the mountaintop, shouting his name in every direction without any success. Even the short distance left her exhausted and panting for breath. Lavender could hardly think straight.

John couldn't have gone that far . . . He could probably hear her but was just too stubborn or too upset by all the fighting to answer back.

Lavender trudged in a circle around the perimeter of the mountain, looking for a clue. There had to be something to tell her which way he'd gone. On the steepest side of the mountain, where there were boulders piled up like children's blocks, she could see imprints in the dirt from all their feet. No wonder they were so drained. They had to have come up the mountain by the most difficult route possible.

Lavender didn't think John would have tried to climb down that way. She kept looking, and on the far side of the peak, she found a few footprints in the dust. He was walking east.

She didn't know why, and she didn't know what he hoped to accomplish, but the footprints in the dirt had to be his. Holding her head in her hands, Lavender walked a few yards, calling his name, and scanning the area. If only she could focus. If only she'd brought her binoculars or something. She found no trace of him other than the fuzzy outline of his sneakers' soles.

"John!'"

She tried calling his name a few more times. Lavender was as irritated as she was exhausted. They didn't have the time or energy to go stumbling after John, but she also knew in her heart that it was wrong to split up. If they were going to find a way to survive, they had to work together, and they had to find John.

She jogged back to camp as quickly as she could, which wasn't very quick at all.

"Rachelle! Marisol!" she called out. "Get out here. We have to go!"

There was a rustle, and Rachelle emerged from the shrubs. "What do you want?" she said.

"Hurry up! We have to keep going."

"What? Why?" asked Rachelle. "Is there a bear?"

"We have to catch up with John if we're going to find him before dark."

"What are you talking about?"

"John. He left. Ran off. We have to catch up with him."

Rachelle rolled her swollen red eyes. "I thought there was an emergency."

"This is an emergency. We have to stop him from going off on his own. Before he gets attacked by animals or—or—"

"If you want to find him, go for it."

"We have to stick together," Lavender said slowly and clearly. "What happened to leave no man behind?"

"He left us. It's different."

"But we all need each other. We've helped each other so many times."

Rachelle snorted. "Last time I checked, we're still stranded in the middle of nowhere without any water. So I don't think we've actually helped each other all that much."

Rachelle trounced back into the bushes. Lavender took a few steps after her. She would drag Rachelle and Marisol out of there if it killed her—or them—but then Lavender hesitated. She didn't want to hurt Marisol. Not again.

For a moment, the mountaintop was perfectly quiet, perfectly still. There was only silence. Lavender looked off into the distance. The world was beautiful. Dramatic gray-blue skies stretched endlessly into purple mountains. She could see trees and mountains and the "Wonderland of Rocks" stretching in their endless columns, making this one of most the incredible sights that Lavender had ever encountered.

But she could also see the sun low on the western horizon, and she could feel the chill in the air as a breeze picked up again, reminding her of nightfall, when temperatures would plummet and they were exposed on a mountain with no shelter.

She couldn't leave John to face the night alone, and there wasn't any more time to argue with Rachelle or to try and coax Marisol out of hiding. Every minute she hesitated was a minute farther that John could get. Lavender had to catch up with him and talk him into returning. He had voluntarily helped her when the flash flood came, and now it was her turn to help him . . . when he really needed it.

She wished she could leave a note. Lavender would have liked to give Marisol and Rachelle details: which direction she was going and when she'd be back and how long they should wait before coming after her. But since she had no real answers and nothing to write with, she settled for cupping her hands and shouting in their direction.

"I'm going to get John. Be right back!"

Lavender waited, hoping for a reply. When none came, she walked east and started following the footprints that led away from camp. She went slowly, because she didn't have the energy to go fast, and also because a little part of her was hoping that Marisol and Rachelle would run after her.

She did hear some scuffling, and then loud voices. But no one called for her. Lavender continued a few more steps in the direction of John's footprints. They were harder to trace than she'd thought they would be—unclear in the dirt and patchy. It didn't help that her muscles ached and her head throbbed.

Lavender wished that she'd been trained how to track animals. She had seen television shows where expert hunters or survivalists knew how to identify animals by their prints and then follow them. Lavender knelt by one series of footprints on the dusty mountain peak and tried to read the story there.

This particular patch of ground zigzagged with sneakers that seemed to be facing toward camp and other prints that looked headed in the exact opposite direction. To her, it looked like John had almost turned around.

If she was right, he was having doubts. Maybe John had run off because, like Marisol, he needed a few minutes alone. He was exhausted, hungry, thirsty, and upset. He was clearly not in his right frame of mind. None of them were. If he was unsure . . . if he didn't actually want to be separated . . . she should be able to catch up with him. She stood and started to walk after him.

"John!" she shouted. "John, come back!"

There was no reply.

She tried again. "John! Answer me!"

This time, Lavender did hear a returning cry. Her call was followed by a shrill, piercing shriek, but it wasn't John. It was Marisol.

27

Lavender spun around and sprinted back to the mountaintop, past the pile of firewood, past the stone fire ring, and then into the shrubs where Marisol and Rachelle had disappeared.

"What's wrong? Where are you?" Lavender yelled as she crashed toward them.

The only answer she got was incoherent, a flurry of shrieks and terrified babbling. All the dangers of the wilderness ran through her mind. Anything could have happened. Marisol could have been attacked by a mountain lion or stung by a scorpion or bitten by a rattlesnake. Or maybe something happened to Rachelle, and Marisol was panicking. Rachelle could have passed out from too little food and water. She could have gone into shock. She could have lost her mind and pushed Marisol off the mountain. Anything could have happened.

"Where are you?!" Lavender called again.

The only answer was another scream, short and shrill. But it did the trick. Lavender pinpointed the direction of the sound and rampaged through the brush.

"Careful!" Rachelle's arm shot out of nowhere and grabbed Lavender just before she could trip over Marisol, who was curled up on the ground, clutching her right leg and whimpering.

"What happened?" Lavender asked, dropping to her knees beside Marisol—all thoughts of John momentarily forgotten.

"Fell," Marisol said on a sob.

"How? When?"

Rachelle knelt next to Lavender. "She was upset and pacing around and trying to decide what to do about . . . well, everything, and when she tried to turn, her foot caught between a couple of rocks and she fell hard."

Okay, Lavender thought, okay, it's just a fall. No big deal. Sure, it hurts, but she's going to be fine. Lavender waited for her heart to slow down.

"I think her ankle might be broken," Rachelle said.

"*What?*" The word was so loud that Lavender heard her own harsh question echo off the surrounding rocks. A broken bone was bad. Marisol couldn't search for water or hike down a mountain with a broken bone. Panicking, Lavender knelt over her friend, trying to ignore the dizzy sensation the sudden movement gave her. "Let me see." Lavender leaned forward and tried to wrench Marisol's hands away from the knee she clutched to her chest.

Marisol winced. The movement jolted her injured ankle, and she screamed again, another short, piercing wail. Desperate to help, Lavender fought to tear Marisol's leg free from her iron grip. Lavender had to help. She had to see if Marisol's ankle was broken.

"Stop it," Rachelle commanded, swatting Lavender away. "Stop it. You're making it worse. You're hurting her."

Rachelle's words cut through her panic. Lavender fell back and stopped trying to force Marisol to release her hurt leg. Marisol remained scrunched up on the gravel, crying, each sob cutting through Lavender like a knife.

"I have to do something," Lavender said.

"The most important thing is to hold the injury still," Rachelle said. "We have to make a splint."

"But I don't know how to make a splint," Lavender wailed.

"I do," said Rachelle.

"It hurts," Marisol moaned again. Dirt streaked her cheeks, her lips were dry and cracked, and her eyes were screwed up tightly in pain.

Lavender looked from Marisol to Rachelle before asking, "Will you make a splint? Can you help her?"

"Of course," Rachelle said. "That's what I'm trying to do if you'll help me."

Lavender moved aside and allowed Rachelle to take over. Speaking in a soft and gentle voice, Rachelle coaxed Marisol into letting go of her leg. In a less gentle voice, Rachelle ordered Lavender to hold Marisol's hands. Marisol's cold fingers clung to Lavender, her nails digging into Lavender's palms, sending a shooting pain into her cut from the splinter.

"The pain in my hand actually helps," Marisol grated out in a strangled voice.

"In *your* hand?" Lavender asked, sure she'd have a row of bloody moon-shaped cuts on her palms when Marisol finally released her.

"Yeah, the pressure is hurting the cactus needles. It's a good distraction—" Marisol stopped short on a groan. Lavender winced. She'd forgotten how the almost-invisible prickles had covered Rachelle's and Marisol's hands.

"Definitely broken," Rachelle announced, having eased the sneaker and sock from Marisol's foot. "No, don't look," Rachelle ordered Marisol. "It'll make you feel worse." But Lavender couldn't help it. She had to see Marisol's ankle for herself. She peeked around Rachelle and then wished she hadn't looked.

The sight made her stomach flip. No one's foot was ever meant to bend in *that* direction. Not ever. It looked like it belonged on a broken doll. Marisol wouldn't be able to hobble a single step, never mind hike down a mountain. It would be impossible.

Lavender thought she'd already reached her lowest point. When they ran out of water. When they found the mountaintop deserted. When Rachelle told the truth about sardines. When John ditched them. But this. This was worse. Waves of pain and panic blossomed. It was getting difficult to breathe. She could hear her rapid breaths, feel the tightening in her chest, and—

"Lavender. Lavender. *Lavender.*" Rachelle's sharp

voice snapped Lavender to attention. "Focus. I said I need you to find a couple sticks."

"Sticks? What sticks?" Lavender gasped.

"Can you loosen your grip?" Marisol asked. Looking at their clasped hands, Lavender was startled to see her friend's fingers looked purple. "When I said the pain helped, I didn't think you would try to break my hand in half."

"Sorry." Lavender dropped Marisol's hands. She could still hear her own unnaturally loud breath. Lavender shook her head and forced herself not to think of anything but the immediate moment. When she regained a little control, she asked Rachelle, "What kind of sticks?"

"If I'm going to make a splint, get something strong. It needs to be sturdy. Just find what you can. We can break them to the right size if they're too big."

"On it." Lavender picked her way out of the shrubs and made a beeline to the firewood she and Marisol had gathered earlier. Surely there would be something there. She sifted through the pile, taking longer than she should. She was tired, confused, and panicking, so the simple task felt overwhelming. After a moment, she gave up entirely on trying to decide for herself. She loaded her arms with as many sticks and twigs as she could hold and tore back to Rachelle, throwing them down at her side. "Are any of these good?"

Rachelle's eyes widened in surprise. "Wow, that's a lot. I'm sure something here will work."

As Rachelle sifted through firewood, Lavender asked, "What else? What else can I do?"

"We need something for padding. Anything we can cushion her foot with. We have one of her socks, and I was going to use my socks but—" Rachelle grimaced and gestured to her feet. For the first time, Lavender noticed that she was barefoot. Rachelle must have removed her shoes and socks while Lavender was getting firewood. And that wasn't the only thing. Rachelle's socks were disgusting—the heels were coated in dark brown and reddish goo. Blood, Lavender realized, some of it drying and dark, some of it fresh and still wet.

"What happened?" Lavender asked.

"I told you my new shoes hurt."

"Your feet." Lavender looked from the socks to Rachelle's feet. Even in the twilight, she could see they looked like raw hamburger.

"I told you to break in new shoes before hiking," Marisol said in a strained voice.

"I thought we were going on a short walk through the desert with our class," Rachelle retorted. "I didn't know I'd be hiking for days."

Lavender couldn't speak. She didn't know what to say. She'd tuned out Rachelle's complaints about her feet and her shoes. They were all suffering, but she hadn't realized . . . If Lavender's feet looked like that, she would have given up hours ago. She would have sat down at the bottom of the mountain and refused to take another step. Lavender could not even begin to imagine how much it must have hurt Rachelle to climb the mountain with feet like that.

As she pulled off her own socks, a feeling of genuine respect for Rachelle washed over Lavender. Maybe she'd never seen any good in Rachelle before because she'd never looked for it. Could it be possible that she'd made up her mind about Rachelle on her first day at school . . . and been wrong? Really, really wrong?

Lavender had never thought that she would admire Rachelle. Not in a hundred million years. It made her think that maybe they would survive this after all. Sometimes the impossible was more possible than you thought. Miracles could happen. And that's what they would need to make it home alive.

28

"We could use my backpack for padding," Lavender said, wishing that John was still around. They could really use his sweatshirt or jacket. But the backpack would have to do for now.

"Good idea," said Rachelle.

Lavender emptied it, and Rachelle used the remaining toilet paper for additional padding. Then Rachelle cradled Marisol's broken foot in the backpack as Lavender took hold of Marisol's hands and tried to keep her from moving as Rachelle placed the sticks alongside everything and then tied it all together with their socks.

Marisol was crying again before they were done. Rachelle's forehead was scrunched into deep grooves, and she looked as upset as Marisol.

"I'm sorry. I'm sorry," Rachelle kept repeating as she immobilized the leg.

Lavender had never felt so useless in her life. She couldn't even offer either of them a drink of water. All she could do was hold on to Marisol and tell Rachelle, "It's okay. Keep going. You're doing the right thing." At least, Lavender hoped Rachelle was doing the right thing. Lavender hadn't ever broken a bone before, and she didn't know a single thing about first aid. By the time Rachelle finished, her hands were trembling, and as she tied off the last sock, she gave Lavender a helpless look. "What now?" she asked.

"C-c-cold," Marisol said. "I'm so cold."

Lavender's instinct was to drag Marisol out of the bushes to the spot where Marisol had cleared space for the fire. A few days ago, or even hours ago, that's exactly what she would have done. But now, simply taking charge didn't feel quite right—

"Rachelle? Marisol?" she heard herself say in a hesitant voice. "Do you think we can get out of the brush? If we move back over that way, we can light a fire. What do you think?"

"I don't know . . ." Rachelle said in a shaken voice.

"I—I want to do it," Marisol said between teeth that chattered.

"Are you sure?" Lavender asked.

"Yes," Marisol said in such a decisive voice that Lavender felt a tiny smile tug at the corners of her mouth. That was Marisol: brave enough to sing a solo in front of a hundred people, fearless enough to pick up a bug that would send anyone else running for cover, and tough enough to face the pain of moving after she'd broken her ankle.

"It's really not a good idea to move a broken bone." Rachelle was actually twisting her hands.

"B-better than freezing to d-death in the bushes," Marisol said.

"Isn't that what the splint is for? To hold it still?" Lavender asked. "Let's just try if that's what Marisol wants. It should be her choice."

At this, Rachelle nodded.

"Y-you guys can be my crutches," Marisol suggested. Her teeth were still chattering, and Lavender wondered if there was something else besides the cold that would cause her to stutter like that.

Marisol held her arms out, and working together, Rachelle and Lavender helped her pull to a standing position. All of Marisol's weight rested on her uninjured leg and on Lavender's and Rachelle's shoulders, and Lavender was relieved when she didn't collapse from the pressure. She was feeling so frail and fragile herself. Then, inch by painful inch, they crept to the clearing.

"Y-you make a good team," Marisol told them.

Once there, they laid Marisol down on the rock. She flinched at the cold, and Lavender wished they still had John's jacket or backpack or anything for Marisol to lie on, but Marisol did not complain. Not even when Rachelle elevated her splinted foot on a rock she'd moved into position.

"You should keep it elevated," she explained. "I think it's supposed to help with swelling."

Then Rachelle gathered more wood as Lavender built up the fire. It was more difficult to start a fire than she would have thought, and it didn't help that she was shivering so hard she couldn't hold her hands steady or that her head was still fuzzy.

Lighting the fire took her a dozen tries before some of the bigger sticks caught. She kept the fire small, hoping to make their scant wood supply last as long as possible. As the last of the evening light faded and darkness settled over the mountain peak, they crowded on either side of Marisol as close to the fire as possible and discussed their options. Both Lavender and Rachelle agreed it was too dangerous to keep hunting for wood . . . or to go after John.

The entire area was treacherous and uneven. The last thing they needed was another broken ankle.

"I hope he's okay," Lavender said softly. It was scary enough to be lost in the wild, but to be completely alone out there . . . She shivered and snuggled a little closer to Marisol.

"Me too." Rachelle's quiet answer surprised Lavender.

"You didn't want to look for him earlier," Lavender reminded her.

"I was—I was—" Rachelle searched for the words.

"Having a moment?" Marisol wheezed in a voice unlike her usual rich tone.

"That's a nice way to put it," said Rachelle. "I was freaking out. I mean, I feel so guilty."

"You feel guilty?" Lavender felt her mouth hanging open in shock. "What do you have to feel guilty about?"

"Are you kidding?" Rachelle said, shaking her head. "I insisted that we should climb the mountain. I was so positive we'd see the campground from up here, or at least a trail. And instead I led us to a dead end. I freaked out. That's part of why I was so upset at you and why I made such a big deal about John and the money. I just wanted someone else to be mad at instead of . . . me."

"Not your fault." Marisol reached up and squeezed Rachelle's hand.

The words were like a knife. "No, it's mine," Lavender said.

Rachelle twisted to look at her. "It kind of is."

"Thanks," said Lavender, "you're making me feel so much better."

"I'm not trying to make you feel better; I'm trying to tell you the truth."

Lavender squirmed and rested her aching head in her arms, uncomfortable because all of this had started with a lie. Her lie.

Rachelle continued. "You shouldn't have tried to trick us. That was really, really mean, but I thought about what John said. He's right. You did save the class with the flood warning, and you came to get me and Marisol."

"Can you guys ever forgive me?" Lavender asked, turning her face toward them.

Rachelle shrugged. "It's up to Marisol."

"You're my friend," Marisol said simply.

"Even after everything I did?"

"Friends until the end."

Rachelle gave a soft snort and said, "If we don't figure something out, the end isn't too far off."

They talked in hoarse, weary voices until Lavender grew dizzy with discarded plans for the morning. They should find water. They should look for John. They should climb down the mountain. They should split up—one of them should stay with Marisol while the other hiked down the mountain and found help. No, they should stay together and make some kind of distress signal.

Finally, they agreed on the latter plan. They would wait until it was light enough to search for firewood safely, and then Rachelle and Lavender would gather up as much as they could—anything flammable—and they would build a massive fire. Hopefully, someone who could help them would spot it. Until they were saved, they would take turns looking for water. Because without water, they might not have to worry about trying to survive another night in the wilderness . . . From everything Rachelle knew about first aid, she didn't think they could make it too many more hours without water.

"How do you know so much?" Lavender asked.

"My mom's a nurse, and I wanted to be one, too. Or maybe a doctor."

"And because of your sister," Marisol added.

"I didn't know you have a sister," Lavender said.

"Yeah," said Rachelle. "She was really sick for a long time. It's one of the reasons we moved back down here. The specialist she needed to be close to was in Phoenix. I spent a lot of time with her in hospitals."

"Is she better now?"

"Yeah. We didn't know if she would get better, but she's in remission now," said Rachelle, "so there's always hope."

"You never talked about it," said Lavender, feeling rocked by this information.

"I know," Rachelle said. "It's not easy to talk about."

Lavender took a deep breath. So many things weren't what they seemed. The older Lavender got, the more complicated life became. She wondered what middle school would hold in store for all of them. If only their signal fire worked.

"Let's sing something," Marisol said, breaking the sudden silence.

All three of the girls were in choir, and even with

hoarse throats and uneven breathing, Lavender thought they sounded beautiful when their voices came together. They chose the *Dear Evan Hansen* song that their teacher had picked for their sixth-grade graduation. They liked it so much they sang it softly three times in a row, and Lavender found herself feeling strangely peaceful on what should have been the most miserable night of her life.

Maybe it was because they had a fire to share. Or maybe it was reaching some kind of real understanding with Rachelle. Maybe it was Marisol's forgiveness. Or maybe it was the song they sang: "You Will Be Found."

29

Somewhere in the night, both Rachelle and Marisol fell into a fitful sleep. Lavender became drowsier and drowsier until even the cold and the hunger and the animal sounds could not keep her awake. Still, she refused to let herself sleep. Someone needed to watch over the others and guard the dying embers of the fire.

Lavender stood. She staggered back and forth. She slapped her own face, pinched her arm, and bit the inside of her cheek: anything to stay awake. The long night stretched on and on, and Lavender could not sleep, would not sleep, and so it was Lavender alone who watched as the clouds overhead broke and the night grew bright with moonlight and starshine. Late in the night, she heard a rustling noise, and

Lavender looked over to see her friend's eyes glitter in the reflected light.

"You awake?" Marisol whispered to her.

Lavender nodded. "Too much on my mind," she said. "How about you?"

"My ankle," Marisol answered. "It really hurts."

"How can I help?" Lavender asked in a whisper so they wouldn't wake Rachelle.

"Having you next to me—knowing we can talk— is enough. At least it gives me something else to think about."

"Then . . . can I ask you a question?"

"Anything."

Lavender bit her lip. She was almost afraid to ask, but if she didn't just say what was on her mind, she might never get a chance. So despite the cold and the hundred aches and pains, she took a deep breath and asked, "Why did you ditch me for Rachelle?"

Marisol was silent for so long that Lavender didn't think she would answer, but then Marisol said, "Just because we're best friends, that doesn't mean we can't have other friends. You never want me to hang out with anyone else. You even joined choir when I did."

"I thought you wanted me to be in choir," Lavender said.

Marisol cocked her head to one side. "Do you really like being in choir?"

"I like to sing. I really do. But I don't love it, not like you do, and choir practice gets really boring sometimes." Lavender paused before adding, "I guess I can think of other things I like better."

"Then you should do those things. We have to be our own people. My mom said that it's healthier to have our own lives."

"I thought your mom liked me. Why would she say that?"

"She does, but I was crying after I failed my ham radio test."

"You took the ham test?"

"I tried and—"

"You should have told me! I could have helped you study. You're so smart. You could easily pass."

"But that's the thing. I didn't really want to do it. I was only trying because you wanted me to take it. And that's when my mom told me that it's okay for us to have some things that belong to just us. She said that I shouldn't always try to do what you do . . . and then, I guess if I'm being one hundred percent honest, I got mad at you, too."

"Why?" Lavender asked with a small shiver.

"You always get all the attention from everyone without even trying or realizing it. You're just always better than me at, like, everything."

"No, I'm not. I can't speak another language. I can't sing like you. I wasn't Alice in the school play. That was you . . ."

Marisol held up a hand and Lavender's voice faded away. Marisol said, "I just mean that, like, singing is my thing. And I was really excited about my solo. If we had just waited, Mrs. Jacobson would have come back and restarted the song. Everything would have been fine, but you jumped to the front and got all the attention, and I was so thrown off by everything that I didn't sing very well, and . . . and I just wanted some space. I probably could have found a better way to talk to you. I didn't want to hurt your feelings exactly, but I was upset and I didn't know what to say. I'm sorry."

A slight breeze stirred the air.

Lavender shivered and edged a little closer to the fire.

Marisol's words were slowly sinking in. As much as Lavender wanted to explain and defend her motives—she'd only been trying to help—maybe Marisol did have a point. In a way, it wasn't that different from what John had said. Sometimes it was better to listen to others than to just jump in and take over.

The silence stretched on until Lavender broke it by clearing her throat.

"And you know I'm sorry, too? Right?" Lavender said. "For tricking you and getting us stranded out here and lying and—and for trying to take over and ruining the concert for you. I really am sorry."

"I know," Marisol said.

"And you really do forgive me?"

"Without forgiveness, no one would ever stay friends."

For an injured sixth grader who was stranded in the woods and on the brink of dehydration and starvation and hypothermia, Marisol was really wise. Lavender felt curiously reassured and whole and safe. And suddenly she wanted to laugh. She shook with silent, semi-hysterical laughter.

Marisol must have felt her moving. "What's the joke?"

"Next time," said Lavender in a voice that still quaked with laughter, "let's not wait until we're about to die to be honest with each other. Like, would we ever have talked if we weren't lost out here?"

"Good point." Marisol gave a little laugh. "It's a deal. Next time, it'll be different."

A cracking twig made Lavender jump, and Marisol inhaled sharply.

"What's that?" Lavender whispered. Marisol lifted her head, trying to look beyond her carefully elevated, restrained foot. Lavender sat up on her knees and scrabbled to grab a handful of rocks. The noise could be anything.

A hulking figure on hind legs emerged from the trees.

"It's a bear!" Marisol rasped out the words.

Drawing back her arm, Lavender threw the handful of pebbles, the only weapon she could locate, at the creature.

The bear raised its arms to shield its face and cried out, "Ow! Stop. It's me."

"John?" Lavender dropped the remaining rocks and rushed over to the shadowy figure. "Is that you?"

"Yeah, it's me. Oof—" John grunted as Lavender launched herself toward him and flung her arms around his middle.

"You came back!"

"I had to," he said. "I found water."

30

As dawn broke, chasing away the last of the night stars, the four shared sips of water from John's bottle. At first, Rachelle wanted to debate whether or not it was safe to drink, and if they should find a way to boil it over the fire. But Lavender decided that if it would help with her headache, she wasn't going to wait for it to boil, and Marisol pointed out that at the moment, dehydration was a bigger threat than just about anything else.

As they drank, John told them that he thought he could retrace his steps to the small stream he'd found. "It's not much," he said. "Just a trickle, probably the last of the mountain snowmelt, but we should get as much into all the water bottles as possible.

And there was a dead tree near the water. We could try to break off some of the branches from the tree and drag them back here for your distress signal."

"Perfect," said Lavender. "You'll need help. Rachelle can go with you. I'll stay here with Marisol . . ." Her voice trailed away as it struck her that maybe she didn't know best. "Or," she said, "maybe Rachelle should stay with Marisol, since she seems to know the most about first aid and her feet could probably use a break. What do you all think?"

After a short discussion, they decided that it made the most sense for Rachelle to stay with Marisol. Rachelle would try to keep the last little embers of their fire from dying out, and hopefully, Lavender and John would return not only with more water but a few big branches.

Together, she and John set out with all four of the water bottles. She was still sore and achy and exhausted, but hope gave her the will to put one foot in front of the other as she followed John. He had marked the way back to the stream with small rock piles, which he called cairns.

"I'm ready to light this entire forest on fire if it means someone will find us," John said as they walked.

Lavender wanted to lecture him about how selfish and irresponsible and dangerous that would be, but in her heart, she felt the same way, so she said nothing. John took her silence the wrong way.

"Are you mad at me?" he blurted out.

"For finding water?" Lavender's stomach rumbled, and she wished that John could also magically stumble across a chicken fried steak with country gravy. Or a bottle of Tylenol.

"No—are you mad at me for leaving? Or for stealing from the class?"

Lavender took a deep breath. "No, I already know why you took the money. It doesn't take a genius to figure out you wanted that money for your bus ticket."

John glanced down at his feet as he guided them past another of the small rock piles. "I never should have done it. It was stupid. And wrong. I knew it was as soon as I'd taken it, but then I was scared to give it back and desperate and angry."

"Is that why you were acting so weird?"

He paused. "I haven't really been myself, I guess. All I could think about was getting away from my parents. Right or wrong, things got so bad, I didn't care."

"Because of how much your parents were fighting," Lavender said, remembering their conversation from the day before. Then it hit her like a photon torpedo. No wonder he'd been so tense every time she and Rachelle snipped at each other. With all the fighting at home, he'd just shut down when he heard other people arguing.

She stopped walking. The sunrise was breaking, and early-morning light was piercing through the pine overhead. John paused beside her.

He nodded and said, "I think my mom and dad hate each other more than they love me and my brother." His voice cracked. "Since my brother left to study abroad, it's been really awful. I just don't have anyone to talk to." He stopped and swallowed hard like he was pushing down a sob. "I don't have the kind of friends I can talk to about stuff like this, and—" He broke off.

Lavender reached out and squeezed his arm. "You do now," she said, and after her talk with Marisol last night, Lavender knew it was true. She had room for more than one friend in her life, and if anyone ever needed a good friend, it was John.

John looked shocked, but then he nodded as a smile spread across his dusty, dirt-smeared cheeks.

He started walking again, leading Lavender around a boulder.

"Just promise me, if we ever make it back to civilization, that you'll talk to me before you try to run away or steal again," she said.

He glanced over his shoulder and gave her a long, hard look before saying, "I can do that." And she believed him, because that's what friends did. They forgave. And they trusted.

They walked a little farther in silence. He was leading them downhill now. The empty water bottles clunked together with each step.

"What happened to the money? Did it all get blown away?" he asked.

"No. I think I picked most of it up," Lavender said. "I haven't counted, but I think it's mostly still there."

"Good. If we get back to school . . . No, I mean, when we get back to school, I'd like to talk to the principal and—"

"No!" Lavender said. "I'll figure it out. I'm going to come up with a way to return the money."

John shook his head. "No, you don't always get to call the shots, remember? It's called teamwork."

Lavender tried, rather heroically, not to roll her eyes. She failed.

John grinned. "I know it's cheesy, but this is my deal. I have to own up to what I did. Hopefully, everyone will be so glad we're alive that they won't throw me in juvie."

"But what can I do?" Lavender asked, following him between two trees to a spot thick with brush.

"If it goes badly, you can visit me in jail."

"You got it," Lavender said, and then she fell silent in reverent wonder as he knelt in the brush and pulled back some branches to reveal a small trickle of water, hidden from view by the foliage. It took her breath away.

Friends, Lavender decided, were like that improbable little stream that was going to save all their lives. They were water in the desert.

31

After filling the water bottles, they returned to camp, carrying and dragging as many branches as possible. The sunbeams on Lavender's face chased away the last of the night chill, and Lavender made a mental note to put on her sunscreen after they got the fire going. Yesterday, they'd at least had some shade under Apache pines. Here on the mountaintop, there were fewer places to hide from the blazing sun. But Lavender kept her complaints to herself.

Tilting her head up, she scanned the empty sky. They needed a plane or helicopter or drone to spot their fire. Because they were out of backup plans. Without help, they would never get Marisol down from the mountain.

"How's that?" Lavender asked John. She and Rachelle had been helping him create a tepee structure that John claimed would make a taller flame.

"Good," John said. "Now we just need to get the embers to catch."

The fire from the night before had almost completely burned itself out. Without a large supply of fuel, they hadn't been able to keep it going all night. And since they'd already burned the driest pieces of wood, the signal fire was going to be even harder to start.

"I found some dead grass we can use for kindling," Rachelle said.

"I think that's a good start," said John. "But if we want these bigger branches to catch, I wish we had more."

"What about the toilet paper from my cast?" Marisol chimed in.

"No," Rachelle said. "We'd have to move your leg, and I don't think we should do that unless we have no other options."

"There's always the envelope and telescope money . . ." Lavender said reluctantly. She didn't really want to burn the class's money, but if it saved their lives, it would be worth it.

"No! Don't do that," John said. Then he smacked his forehead. "You know what? I think I have some papers in my backpack. We could burn those."

Lavender remembered the maps and bus schedule she'd seen yesterday.

As Rachelle piled her handful of leaves and twigs at the base of the firewood, Lavender poked the black ash from last night's blaze, searching for any red embers.

"Maybe you should try the lighter," Rachelle suggested.

Lavender pulled the lighter from her back pocket and was just touching it to Rachelle's kindling as John said, "Got it." She heard the sound of paper crumpling, and then he said, "Here, this'll do the trick." He tossed the papers into the fire ring.

As the edge of the closest paper—one of the maps— caught, John held something out to Lavender. She glanced away from the flame to see it was a couple of hair ties.

"These were in the front pocket. I forgot I had them," he said.

Lavender reached out and took them. "What?"

Something important was niggling at the edges of Lavender's brain. She gave her head a little shake. If only her mind wasn't so muddled.

"You dropped them on the bus," John reminded her.

Like lightning, it all came together. The hair ties weren't the only thing she'd dropped. The paper. The note from her dad. Where was it?

Without thinking, Lavender reached into the fire.

"What are you doing?" Rachelle shrieked.

"Careful!" John shouted at the same time.

The bus schedule and the maps were completely consumed, but the last paper—the one with the distinctive black letters in all caps—had landed a little farther from the flames. Fire was licking the edge of that last paper, and it singed Lavender's fingers as she snatched it out of the flames and dropped it in the dirt.

"Stamp it out!" Marisol called to her.

That was the first sensible thing anyone had said or done since Lavender stuck her hand in the fire. Lavender smothered the flame with the bottom of her shoe.

"What did you do that for?" Rachelle cried out.

"She obviously needed the paper," Marisol said.

It was so good to hear her best friend defend her that Lavender smiled. "I saw my dad's handwriting," she explained. "He said he put a note in my backpack, but I lost it. I dropped it on the bus without ever reading it." Lavender choked over the last words.

Lavender bent to pick up the paper. It was dusty and wrinkled. The note had been folded and unfolded and then wadded up and singed by fire. As she reached for it, she noticed that her own hands weren't faring much better. She barely recognized them. They were cut and scraped. Her right palm was still crusted in dried blood from the splinter even after trying to rinse it off in the stream. The dirt and ash under her fingernails were pitch black. But none of that mattered as she smoothed out her dad's note.

FREQUENCY: 146.420 MHz
NEGATIVE SHIFT (OFFSET -0.6 MHz)
PL TONE: 162.2
TALK SOON. LOVE YOU, DAD

That was all it said, but it was enough.
"I need my radio," Lavender said.

32

"**Haven't we already** tried this?" Rachelle asked with a little huff.

"Shhhhh," Lavender ordered. Her stomach was flipping and her hands were shaking worse than ever before. She felt like she might fly into a hundred pieces. Hope was terrifying. She was afraid to explain, afraid to try, afraid of the crushing disappointment if this didn't work.

"What was in the note?" Marisol asked for the third or fourth time.

"It looks like gibberish to me," John said. Lavender could feel him leaning over her shoulder to read it.

"It's everything we need to talk into the repeater," Lavender said, frantically programming her radio.

"Still gibberish," Rachelle said.

"My dad gave me the repeater settings so I could talk with him in Phoenix."

"English, Lavender. Speak English," Marisol commanded.

They weren't going to leave her alone until she explained. With a sigh, Lavender tore her eyes from the radio. "A repeater is kind of like an antenna that takes a weak radio signal and boosts it. I haven't been able to reach anyone with my radio, because it has a small antenna and not a lot of power. Kind of like how John's phone won't work, because we don't have a cell signal. A repeater is just like a cell tower. But a radio repeater will transmit our signal. Even though this radio is small, it will reach a lot farther than a cell phone. My dad told me we could talk through the repeater, but without the right settings, it was hopeless."

Marisol shook her head. "What are you saying?"

"I'm saying"—she took a long breath, trying to steady herself—"I'm saying, we might be saved."

Rachelle knelt beside Lavender on the ground, clutching her arm. "Are you serious? You think you can, like, actually call someone on that thing. For real this time?"

"I think so." Lavender nodded and held down the talk button.

Lavender held down the talk button.

Whatever she said would be rebroadcast for everybody to hear. Other radio operators for dozens and dozens of miles would be able to hear her message.

"Help," she said. The word was dry and cracked. She suddenly had no breath to say the words. Her finger slipped from the talk button.

"Here." John produced Lavender's water bottle and handed it to her. She took a few sips. "You've got this."

Calm down, be calm, Lavender coached herself. You outran a flood, escaped from a bear, and climbed a mountain. You can figure this out.

But reaching out and asking for help, it felt like the scariest thing that had happened so far. Because if this didn't work . . . if there was no one listening . . . if she was wrong about the repeater . . . if she couldn't contact anyone . . . this might be the thing that finally broke her beyond repair. To have this much hope and be disappointed. She didn't think she could recover.

Lavender took a deep breath, held down the talk button, and this time she spoke with more conviction.

"This is KG7XAB. I am lost in the Chiricahua Wilderness with three of my classmates. This is an emergency."

She let go of the talk button, waited, and heard the beep that indicated she had actually contacted the repeater.

Now she just needed someone to be listening. Someone had to be out there. They just had to.

"Mayday, Mayday," she transmitted again. "Please, please answer me. This is KG7XAB. I am stranded in Chiricahua with my friends. We got separated from our class after a flash flood. We need help. It's an emergency."

Only static filled the little radio.

With every second, every crackle, Lavender felt a little piece of her heart start to die.

And then—"This is KB7XWT. I hear your distress."

Lavender was so startled she dropped her radio. "We're saved! We're saved! You guys, we're saved!" She clapped and jumped around in an impromptu jig that made her head pound. She didn't even care. This had to be one of the best moments of her life.

"You did it!" John grabbed her shoulders and shook them. "You really did it."

Rachelle jumped on them in a group hug.

"Come in, come in," the faint voice crackled over the radio. "This is KB7XWT. Come in."

"Lavender!" Marisol shouted from her spot on the ground. "Focus. We're not home yet."

Lavender, John, and Rachelle broke apart, startled out of their celebration by Marisol's reality check.

"Is anyone there?" the man's voice spoke again.

Lavender dove for the radio, scraping her elbows, and mashed down on the transmitter. "Come in, KB7XWT. This is KG7XAB. My name is Lavender. I'm on a mountain in Chiricahua Wilderness. We were at our sixth-grade science campout, and we got separated from the rest of group by a flash flood. Please, please send help."

"You're really the missing schoolkids?" he said. "You've been all over the news. Folks around here have been awfully scared that you didn't make it out of that flood, but your dad asked for volunteers to listen to this frequency twenty-four/seven until you were located."

Lavender's eyes prickled, thinking of her mom and dad. They never would have quit looking for her, but they might have given up hope that she would be alive when they found her. They would be so happy when they heard she was okay, probably even happier than she was to get away from this mountain . . . if that was possible.

"Can you tell my parents I'm all right?" Lavender said. "We're hungry and dirty and injured, but we're alive. I'll give you their phone number if you'll just tell them I'm alive."

"You'll tell them yourself, kid. Help is on the way."

33

From there, everything moved both too fast and too slow all at once. The search and rescue workers couldn't just materialize on the mountaintop. First, they had to locate Lavender and her friends, based on their descriptions of the area. As Lavender tried to answer their questions, John and Rachelle built up the fire so their rescuers would have a signal to guide them to the right mountain peak.

Lavender heard the helicopter before she saw it, and no sound was ever sweeter than the chop of the helicopter blades when their rescuers arrived.

In her excitement, Lavender dropped the radio again. She jumped up and down, waving her arms. Rachelle and John joined her, and even Marisol from her spot on the ground waved both arms like her life depended on it.

It felt like an eternity for the helicopter to maneuver into position. Huge gusts of wind from the copter's blades turned the mountaintop into a hurricane. Then a man on a rope and harness was floating down, down, down toward them. When the man was firmly on the ground, Rachelle pointed and shouted, "Take Marisol first. She's hurt. Broken ankle, I think."

And then the man was walking toward them and shouting back that it was hard to hear through his helmet, so Rachelle should just keep talking as loud as she could.

Once he understood, their rescuer stabilized Marisol's leg before hooking her to himself in a thing like a big vest that connected them both to a cable, and then they were pulled into the helicopter. Lavender was the last one to get taken up. She insisted on it.

As the man in the jumpsuit helped Lavender into the harness, he said, "Just stay nice and calm. Keep your arms tucked in. Don't try to grab anything."

His warning almost sounded like the workers at amusement parks who told people to keep their arms inside the ride at all times. The helicopter moved back into place, and the man in the tan jumpsuit hooked them onto the rope with a big metal clip, and Lavender suddenly pictured the clip breaking or the cable snapping. Surely, they could have found some other way to rescue her.

With a yank, they were airborne. As they rose up toward the helicopter, they spun and twisted. Lavender felt like she was riding the teacups at Disneyland while flying through the air. She squeezed her eyes shut, not wanting to watch as the trees shrank into toothpicks. *Don't vomit, don't vomit, don't vomit*, she ordered herself. If she'd made it this far, she could survive the rescue, too.

Then a woman in a matching tan jumpsuit was pulling her farther into the helicopter and asking her if she was okay and handing her water. Lavender took small sips. The water was pure and clean. She could feel it rinsing away the grit that lined her mouth— her teeth felt like they were full of dust and sand after days of sleeping outside and drinking dirty water.

John, Marisol, and Rachelle were tucked into different corners of the crowded helicopter. They looked as pale and shell-shocked from the ride as she felt.

"We're taking you to the hospital. Your parents are being notified. They will meet you there." The man shouted to be heard.

"She's the only one who needs a hospital," John shouted back, pointing at Marisol.

The woman and Rachelle shook their heads at the same time.

"We want to have you checked out. You were out there a long time," the woman answered.

"We sure are glad you found a way to contact us," the man hollered again.

"Everyone was afraid you had drowned," the woman said. "And one girl from your class swore you'd climbed out of the wash on the opposite side from here."

"Does that mean everyone else was okay?" John yelled to be heard.

The man nodded. "Yep, the others backtracked to a trail, and one of the teachers eventually got a phone signal."

"We've been searching for you ever since they called us," the woman added.

A chill ran up Lavender's spine. She was relieved that the rest of the sixth grade was safe, but she couldn't stop thinking about how close they'd come to never being found.

But they were rescued. And they were going to see their families. These people in the helicopter had dropped everything to come and pluck Lavender and her friends off the top of a mountain.

Lavender turned to the lady who was closest to her.

"Thank you," she said.

≈

No shower ever felt better than the tiny, sterile hospital shower with the astringent shampoo and body wash. No bed ever felt softer. No pillow more wonderful. Lavender and the other three stayed overnight at the hospital with their moms and dads, too. All their parents had been helping comb the park, looking for their lost children. And none of them were going to let their kids out of sight for a long, long while.

After being fed and fussed over by about a hundred doctors and nurses and medical assistants, Lavender sat on her hospital bed while her mom combed the tangles from her hair, occasionally finding a small leaf or twig.

"You might need to shower again," her mom said.

Lavender wrinkled her nose. "At home," she said. "I'm too tired now."

Her mom agreed. Both of her parents had asked her a barrage of questions, and Lavender had answered, skimming over some of the details because her mom started to sniffle in a heartbroken way when the story got too intense.

Her dad's phone buzzed continuously as they talked. Friends, relatives, neighbors . . . everyone was sending texts and getting in touch to make sure that Lavender really was okay, to say how happy they were that she'd been found, and things like that.

After one message, her dad looked up and said, "That was the *Today* show."

"The news show?" Lavender asked.

"They want to fly you and your classmates out to New York for an interview."

"Whoa," said Lavender, impressed with herself and her friends. "That's the other side of the country."

"I don't know," said her mom, gently working at a stubborn tangle. "I don't like all this publicity focused on such young kids."

Her dad nodded thoughtfully. "We'll have to talk to the other parents about the best way to handle this."

"But, Dad," said Lavender, "at least promise that I can talk to *QST* magazine if they want to do a story."

"The ham radio magazine?" her mom asked.

"Yes," said Lavender. "It saved a lot of lives. First with the flood, and then getting us down from the mountain."

Her dad chuckled. "I think we can let you do at least one interview."

Her mom finished combing out Lavender's hair, and then Lavender crawled under the covers, and in the quiet of a little room with her parents on either side, Lavender slept in safety and warmth, and it was the most perfect night of sleep she could ever remember.

Best of all, both of her parents were still there when she woke up again.

≈

The next day, as they were waiting to be discharged, John stopped by Lavender's hospital room to ask if she would help him study for his ham radio license.

"Really?" she said. "You really want to take the test? You have to learn a lot about radios and electronics."

"That sounds interesting to me. I've always liked science."

"Cool." Lavender smiled.

"John, come on. The doctor's on his way to your room. Your dad's waiting." John's mom appeared in the doorway and put her arm around her son. She gave Lavender a little wave and then took John back to his room, and that's when

Lavender knew that John was going to be okay.

His parents were there for him. Both of them. He'd been wrong about one thing: They loved him more than whatever problems they were having. And, even if things weren't going to be perfect at home, he had friends who would stand by him no matter what.

At last, the final discharge papers were signed, and the families headed out to the parking lot. The parents had decided to caravan back to Phoenix, but as they went for their cars, they were ambushed by reporters.

Lavender heard her mother groan; Lavender herself felt like groaning as Rachelle stepped confidently up to the news camera. Unsurprisingly, Rachelle and her mom were pushing hard for all four kids to accept the offer from the *Today* show. Rachelle looked like her old self again, just a little sunburned. While the others were dressed in comfortable clothes—sweatpants or gym shorts and T-shirts—Rachelle wore skinny jeans, a flowy blouse, designer flip-flops, and a silver necklace. Her curly hair was pulled back in a beautiful thick braid.

Lavender held her breath, fully expecting Rachelle to throw her under the bus. Rachelle would tell about the stupid sardines prank. Lavender had a quick flashback to the concert, when Marisol and Rachelle had called her names. Well, if Rachelle had any lingering resentment, this was her chance to get even with Lavender once and for all.

"How do you feel?" the reporter was asking Rachelle.

"I just feel so glad to be alive and to have taken a shower and slept in a bed," Rachelle said. She put a hand on Marisol's shoulder. Marisol was balanced on crutches. She had an appointment with an orthopedic surgeon in Phoenix set for the next day.

Here it comes, Lavender thought, sinking into her mom's side and bracing for whatever Rachelle might say next.

"But, most of all," Rachelle said, "I am grateful that Lavender was able to save us all. First, she warned the rest of our class about the coming flood. If she hadn't heard the warning on her radio, the entire class might have been washed away because we took a wrong turn on the hike."

Marisol nodded. "And then when she figured out how to talk to the repeater, she was able to use her ham radio to call for help. She's the real hero."

John stayed silent in the background, but he was nodding, too.

Lavender felt her face heat with embarrassment as the entire barrage of people—hospital personnel, parents, and reporters—turned to look at her.

"So you saved the day?" one lady with a microphone asked, turning toward Lavender.

Part of her wanted to brag. Before all of this, that's exactly what she would have done. But she was different now. Facing life and death did that to a person.

Lavender stepped away from her mom, took a deep breath, and squared her shoulders. "Actually," she said, "everyone helped. We were a team. John was so prepared. He had all these supplies in his backpack that probably saved our lives. Marisol had the idea to eat prickly pear when none of us thought we could go any farther. Rachelle knew exactly how to make a splint when Marisol got hurt. And we all worked together to scare off the bear." There was a gasp from right behind her, and Lavender remembered she hadn't shared that little detail with her mom yet. Lavender paused and then she added, "You know what? In the end, it really wasn't just one of us. I didn't save the day. We all saved each other."

And if that wasn't friendship, Lavender didn't know what was.

ACKNOWLEDGMENTS

Grandma Jo inspired me to become a teacher. She is also the first person who told me that I should write a book. In a way, the last fifteen years of my life are all her fault. I am deeply grateful.

My family is a constant source of support. I especially appreciate the unending encouragement from my mom and also from my sister, who has read more versions of this story than should have ever been inflicted on any living creature. My nieces, Daphne and Julia, have been two of my biggest cheerleaders, and I appreciate their enthusiasm.

Thoughtful feedback from The Charglings has helped me tremendously. Thank you, Keith, Laura, Glynka, and Karen, for your invaluable insights.

I sincerely appreciate the faculty, students, and staff at James Madison Preparatory School. I am particularly grateful to Deb for always believing in me as a writer. I owe a debt of gratitude to the 2018–2019 Lambert Homeroom for their input. I am equally indebted to my 2019–2020 seventh-grade classes, whose excitement for this story inspired and motivated me.

Certain elements of this book were far beyond my area of expertise, and I am so grateful to Dad and Bill for giving me advice on all things ham radio and also to Jamie for helping me make an implausible weather event feel possible.

For nearly twenty years of friendship and encouragement even when writing was just a pipedream, I am grateful to Megan, Laura, Annah Kate, Molly, Abbi, and Kim.

The wonderful community from the Vermont College of Fine Arts has shaped my writer's journey. In particular, I would like to thank the faculty and students from the 2018 Bath Spa Residency, where I worked on a version of this manuscript. I would also like to thank Shae, who is a willing sounding board for my writing ideas.

Linda Camacho is an amazing agent. I feel so lucky to be working with her and the entire team at Gallt & Zacker Literary Agency.

Last of all, a huge thank-you to everyone at Scholastic who helped to transform this story and to create such an exciting book design. Most especially, thank you to my editor, Emily Seife, who saw this novel's potential. Without her vision and passion, *Distress Signal* would never have been written.

ABOUT THE AUTHOR

Mary E. Lambert grew up going on ham radio campouts with her family in the mountains of Arizona. While she was never lost and stranded in the wilderness as a result of these trips, she did often think that school, especially fifth and sixth grade, felt like a fight for survival. Today, Mary lives in Tempe, Arizona, where she teaches middle and high school classes at a local charter school. She has often helped chaperone the junior-class camping trip and has assisted in fending off skunks and squirrels, but to date there have been no bear encounters. In 2014, Mary earned her MFA in Writing for Children and Young Adults from Vermont College of Fine Arts. Her first novel, *Family Game Night and Other Catastrophes*, was published in 2017.